Frances Hodgson Burnett

Giovanni and the other; children who have made stories

Frances Hodgson Burnett

Giovanni and the other; children who have made stories

ISBN/EAN: 9783337215446

Printed in Europe, USA, Canada, Australia, Japan

Cover: Foto ©Andreas Hilbeck / pixelio.de

More available books at **www.hansebooks.com**

FRANCES HODGSON BURNETT

GIOVANNI TOOK HIS USUAL BOYISH POSE WITH HIS HANDS ON HIS HIPS

GIOVANNI
AND THE OTHER

Children Who Have Made Stories

BY

FRANCES HODGSON BURNETT

NEW YORK
CHARLES SCRIBNER'S SONS
1897

TROW DIRECTORY
PRINTING AND BOOKBINDING COMPANY
NEW YORK

PREFACE

ALL my life I have made stories, and since I was seven years old I have written them. This has been my way of looking at life as it went by me. Every one has his own way of looking at things. A man or woman who is an artist probably sees everything as a picture. Sunset and sunrise, country and town groups, children playing, older people at work, perhaps all form themselves into pictures when an artist looks at them.

In the same way it happens that scenes, incidents, and persons quite naturally suggest to me the story which may belong to them. I do not know how many such stories pass through my mind in a day. Some of them merely flit through like birds across the sky, and are forgotten, but there are some that stay, or at least leave traces. And in thinking of this once, I found I could call out of the shadows a number of children, some of whom, though only seen for a few moments, have remained quite distinct memories to me, and seem like little friends I like to think about. There are so many of them, of so many countries, speaking such different languages, wearing such different costumes, and each one of them seeming to suggest a story of his own. Sometimes it may be the story of a tiny news-boy in New York; a little fellow with sun-bleached hair whom I find in the mountains of North Carolina; a poor little man waiting in the mud and drizzling rain in a crowded London street, and rushing to open my carriage door in the hope of being given a few coppers; a beautiful little soft-eyed, curly-haired beggar in Rome, lingering in the sun until I drive out of the court-yard of my hotel, that he may run after me, laughing, as he cries out, "*Soldi, Signora!*"—quite sure that he is so pretty and coaxing that he need not pretend to be miserable (which he is not at all), and that the *soldi* will be thrown tinkling onto the pavement. It may be the story of any of these or of many others, but each one is part of some story, and there seems to be a little sketch of each hung in a certain gallery in my mind.

Remembering that to my own childhood the story of a child who was a real, living creature had a special fascination, I have put some of these sketches into words, trying to give them the color which surrounded them and made them stories and pictures to me, thinking that perhaps other children may like to read of small creatures who were as real as themselves, and not only beings of the imagination.

FRANCES HODGSON BURNETT.

CONTENTS

LIST OF ILLUSTRATIONS

GIOVANNI AND THE OTHER

GIOVANNI AND THE OTHER

I

GIOVANNI walked up the enclosed road leading to the great white hotel with the many marble balconies. It was quite a grand hotel and stood in a garden where palm-trees and orange-trees and flowers grew. A white balus-traded terrace separated the garden from the carriage drive by the grey-green olives, and roses and heliotropes grew in tumbling masses over the stone. It was on an elevation, and below it one could see the promenade by the sea and the great lake-like sapphire blue expanse of the Mediterranean.

There were palm-trees and flowers bordering the promenade, and even in the winter there were numbers of children walking about with baskets full of violets and narcissus and anemones, which they ran after the pedestrians with, in the hope of selling.

The sun seemed always shining and the air soft there, and there were always flowers, for the

little town was a pretty quaint one on the Ri-
viera. It was called San Remo, and in the winter was always full of foreigners who came to
see the sun when it seemed finally to have left
England, or to escape from wind and cold when
they were delicate.

Most of them — the *forestieri* — were more or
less delicate. Some of them had thin, pale faces,
and coughed and walked slowly, some of them
were pulled about in invalid rolling chairs, and
often one saw one in deep mourning, and might
guess either that some one belonging to them
had come to the south to get well and had died
in the midst of the flowers and palms and orange-
trees, or that having lost some one they loved in
some other place, had come to try to bear the
shock of their grief in the land where the sunshine
might help them a little.

But whatever had happened to bring them,
whether they were well or ill, or burdened with
sorrow, they always were pleased with two
things. They always were pleased with the
flowers and carried them about in bunches, and if
any one played the guitar and mandolin and sang
well they were pleased, and gave money to the
players and singers.

So there were many flower sellers in the streets
and many flower shops in the town, and there
were many people who wandered about with

mandolins and guitars, playing before the hotels, and generally having with them some one who either could sing sweetly or who tried to. In the latter case sometimes they got money to induce them to go away—to the next hotel, at least.

Giovanni was one of those who fortunately *could* sing, and a man went with him who played the harp.

He was a handsome Italian boy about fourteen years old. He was strong and plump and well-built, and had a dark-eyed, merry, pretty face, and a gay, bright smile. It was rather a lovable face, and when money was thrown to him from the balconies, and he ran and picked it up, pulling off his cap and saying, "Grazie, Signora," or "Signorina," or "Signore," as the case might be, his quick little bow was often returned by a nod.

They had so much money, these *foresticri*, Giovanni thought they might well be good-natured. Think what lives they must have, these people who were rich enough to travel away from unpleasant weather, and who lived in the great gay hotels, eating wonderful things three times a day, waited upon by dozens of servants, and with an imposing *concierge* in uniform and gold buttons, who appeared on the broad, white marble, flower-bordered entrance steps, and, calling up a waiting carriage with a majestic wave of the hand and a

loud "Avante," carried out to it wraps and cushions, and held the door open while the signoras
entered, touching his gold-banded cap gracefully
as they drove away. Ah! what a life it must be,
to be sure.

But though he was only a little peasant, Giovanni knew that fortune had not been so unkind
to him after all. He had his voice, and had had
luck with it ever since the man with the harp had
proposed that he should go and sing with him
before the hotels and villas. Giovanni had a
share of the money, and he was comfortably fed
and given warm clothes, even to the extent of
having a scarf to wrap round his throat on chilly
nights, for fear he should catch cold and become
hoarse. The man with the harp knew he was
worth something.

He had a full, sweet, strong voice, and he sang
his songs of the people with a melodious freshness. He had a little *répertoire* of his own, and
was not reduced to singing "Santa Lucia" as
often as many of the street troubadours. There
was a little song of a reproachful lover who
rather embarrassingly recalls the past to his unkind fair one. "When I am far away," he says,
"you will remember the kisses you have given
me. Yes, you will remember then," etc.

And Giovanni used to stand with his hands on
his hips and pour forth these reproaches in his

clear, full, boyish voice, looking so happy and young and content that it was very charming. And then there was "O je Carolie," and the Riti-rata, and the gayest one of all—a rattling little one—about the Bersaglieri—the dashing sharp-shooters who went "double quick" through life in their picturesque cloaks and broad-brimmed hats on one side, with the great plumes of cock's feathers sweeping their shoulders.

"The Bersaglieri have feathers on their hats," he sang in Neapolitan dialect. "How many little capons and hens have to be destroyed to provide all this beauty. Love the Bersaglieri—love them—they are the saviours of your country." And all so gaily and with such a swing to the air that one could imagine a Bersagliere hearing him would rush forward and shower upon him unlimited soldi.

The morning my story begins with was a perfect one. It was in January, but San Remo was flooded with brilliant sunshine, the Mediterranean was like a great sapphire, the air was as soft as if it had been May. Giovanni was in a joyous humor—but then he usually was—as he and the man with the harp mounted the long flight of stone steps which led into the hotel garden.

"I wonder how much we shall get," he said to his companion. "The Grand Hôtel des Anglais has not been so full this month." That was the

name of the hotel they were going to sing and
play before.

The man with the harp planted it in a good
position before the long flight of broad white
marble entrance steps. There were big pots of
palms and azaleas and flowering plants of various
sorts on each side of the steps all the way up to
the glass door which one of the servants always
stood behind, ready to open.

Giovanni took his usual boyish pose with his
hands on his hips and began to sing. He sang
the song of the reproachful lover and the Bella
Sorrentina, and in the middle of the last he heard
a window open. This was a sound always to be
noted, because it meant that some one was coming
out on to the balcony to listen and would probably throw him some money. But he was artist
enough not to look up until his song was finished.
Even if money was thrown he did not move until
his song was over. Then he used to run and
pick it up, lifting his cap in recognition.

When he had finished La bella Sorrentina he
glanced over the front of the hotel. There were
several balconies which belonged to the larger
apartments, to the people who had suites of two
or three rooms and private *salons*. At the end of
one of these a lady was standing leaning against
the marble balustrade and resting her forehead
on her hand as she looked down at him.

Giovanni saw that she was one of the *foresticri* who were in deep mourning. She was all black but that she had blonde hair which the morning sun was shining on. There was something sad and fatigued about her attitude, and as he looked up she touched her eyes lightly with the finger of the hand that shaded them; with the other hand she made a motion to Giovanni. She held a tiny white package in it. It was some money folded in a piece of paper so that it could be easily seen and found where she threw it.

Giovanni went and stood under her balcony. She smiled down at him and threw the bit of paper with a sort of friendly, almost caressing, gesture which made him feel that she had liked his voice very much, and which caused him to lift his cap with spirit and call out with more than usual feeling his "Grazie, Signora."

Then he ran back to the harp—put the white paper into the harpist's pocket, without looking at it or opening it at all—which was really quite dignified artistic taste for a boy street singer— and he began the song about the Bersaglieri. The lady in black rested against the marble balustrade again and shaded her eyes with her hand.

As she did so a tall girl came out upon the balcony and stood close to her. She was a girl with a lovely rounded face and black-lashed grey eyes.

"What a beautiful voice!" she exclaimed enthusiastically. "What a darling, full, sweet boy voice! What a good voice! And how well he sings."

"He has a dear boy face, too," said the other. "He looks so bright and happy. He looks about as old as Geof, I think. He has just sung one of Geof's songs, 'La bella Sorrentina;' you know he sings that."

The girl gave her a soft, quick, side glance, and drew closer to her, touching her caressingly.

"Don't, dear," she said; "you must not have tears in your eyes."

"Well," answered the lady in black, quietly, and looking over the olives at the sea, "it is so strange how every moment something *reminds* me. Everything makes me remember something—the palm trees and oranges and flowers that we hoped *he* would be strong enough to be brought to see—the Mediterranean that he used to plan to use his launch on—ah! *everything* has some connection of thought with him—and when that boy began, it brought back the days when Geof used to stand singing with his hands on his hips—and how *he* used to sit near and listen and think it was so clever. He used to say, 'Oh, Geof can sing. He's got a voice—but I couldn't do it. I never saw such a fellow as Geof; he can do anything.' You know he always admired Geof's gifts, in a boyish way. And I could not help thinking that if—if all the stories are quite true, the stories of the Far Country where he has gone —perhaps now he sings, too."

She drew her palm softly and quickly across her cheek.

" It makes me feel as if I loved that little fellow down there," she said. " Boys always seem near to me, you know. There, he has finished singing and they are going."

That was the beginning of Giovanni's acquaintance with the lady in black.

II

HE used to come back to sing before the hotel twice a week, and always after the first few bars of his song she used to appear on the balcony and lean on the marble and listen, and watch him. He was always sure of having his silver franc thrown down, folded in paper. On the morning of the Flower Corso, at the end of the Carnival, she threw him two, and often the girl with the grey eyes threw him one also. They never threw him coppers, and they generally waved their hands to him and said, "Buon giorno," as he picked up his money.

Whether money was thrown from other balconies or not he was always sure of his little revenue from the one where the black figure stood listening.

Being a bright, spirited boy who liked to be appreciated, he began to rather look forward to his mornings before the hotel. He felt somehow as if these ladies liked him and were his friends. He began even to feel that he had a sort of claim upon them, and he always sang his best under their balcony and made his most graceful bow.

One day they were walking through the town and a boy passing them stepped aside from the narrow pavement, and pulling off his cap said brightly,—

" Buon giorno, Signore."

The tall girl turned to look at him.

"Ah," she said, "that is our boy who sings. He is alone and he knew us and said 'Buon giorno.' "

The lady in black turned also. " Yes, it is our boy," she said. "Ah, let us go back and talk to him a little. I want to see him closer."

To Giovanni's surprise they turned back and came towards him. He stopped and pulled off his cap again. He had a smooth, pretty dark-haired head, and seen close to he was a handsome boy with a merry smiling face.

" You sing for us before our hotel, don't you ? " said the grey-eyed girl, speaking Italian.

" Si, Signorina," he answered, feeling pleased at her gentle, friendly manner.

" What is your name ? "

" Giovanni Calcagni."

" And you are fond of music ? "

"Si, si, Signorina," smiling.

Then they asked him how old he was and where he had learned to sing, and he told them he was fourteen and had always sung little songs; but about three years ago a one-eyed man had taken him about with him to sing before the villas and hotels, and so he had learned to sing better.

"The Signora here," said the tall girl, "has a boy who is fourteen years old, like you, and he has a beautiful voice and sings some of our Italian songs, so the Signora likes to hear you sing, very much."

"Is the Signorino in San Remo?" Giovanni asked.

"No, he is not in San Remo. He is in America."

Giovanni had heard of America. It was far away. A long voyage across the sea. People went there and became rich. There had been a San Remese sailor, quite a common man, who had gone there, and after two years had come back and built a wonderful villa by the sea. It was a marvellously ornamented villa, fantastically decorated. Giovanni had once heard that there were *forestieri* who smiled at it and said it was decorated like a wedding cake. But it was known to have cost a great deal of money, and the owner had made all this money in America, though no one knew how. Probably he had picked it up in the streets.

This made the lady in black and her friend additionally interesting. They were of course rich, as they lived at the Grand Hôtel des Anglais and threw out silver to singers. But it was more than interesting to hear of a boy of his own age who lived in America and also sang "La bella Sorrentina," and the rest, in Italian. It seemed enviable.

The lady in black looked at him with longing in her eyes, and she gave him a franc for himself on the spot, and then the two smiled and left him.

"I wonder," said the lady in black, as they walked along the promenade under the palm trees, "I wonder if he will have a fine voice when he is a man. It is difficult to tell, I suppose; I have always heard so. Musicians always advise me not to let Geof use his voice too much now he is growing older."

"That is the great point, I believe," said her companion. "Giovanni's voice is a beautiful one, but it may not be so fine when it changes into a man's voice—certainly it won't if he strains it by singing too much now and by forcing his notes."

"It would be a cruel thing for it to be spoiled," returned the lady in black, reflectively. "Think what a future it might make for him if, when he is a young man, he had that splendid gift."

"Now you are making a story out of him," said the girl, with a caressing little laugh. "You are imagining he may have a career before him and be a world-renowned tenor. I know your little ways."

The lady in black smiled.

"Yes," she answered, "of course. I am a romantic person, and I will have my story whenever there is a shadow of a chance. See what a story it would be, Gertrude. Here he is—Giovanni, a perfectly simple, ordinary little peasant boy, singing about the streets with a one-eyed man and a harpist, and feeling quite rich when one throws him a franc. I have no doubt he thinks it is quite splendid to be one of the *foresticri* and live in a hotel. He probably lives in one of the queer old, old tumbling-down houses in the 'Città Vecchia'—one of those in the climbing streets which are like corridors, and have little archways thrown from house to house, and apparently no windows, only tiny square holes, with rusty bars across. You remember how dark they are, and how green things grow out of the stones, and how sometimes there are sheep or cows in the room on the first floor.

"We will suppose he lives there, and sits with the sheep when it is cold. He eats polenta and farinata and castagnone — those brownish and yellowish slabs which look like uninviting pudding when one sees them being cooked over the charcoal fires in the narrow streets. They are made of maize or chestnut flour, and it does not give one an appetite to look at them. Sometimes he has macaroni and goat cheese, and in the summer he eats ripe figs and grapes and black bread. Perhaps he never had a franc all to himself until I gave him that one to-day. I wonder what he will do with it? Perhaps he will buy that hard, sticky cake made of nuts. He looks like a dear boy, but I don't think he looks imaginative or ambitious. I don't imagine he dreams about a career. Now, imagine that this beautiful boy's voice changes into a wonderful tenor. Imagine that some one helps him to cultivate it, and brings him before the world, and it begins to applaud and adore him."

"It would be like a fairy story," said Gertrude; "he would think he was living in a dream."

"He would be rich," said the lady in black. "He would travel from country to country, and everywhere he would be fêted and caressed. Of course we are imagining him to be a sort of king of tenors, and not one with an ordinarily good voice. Kings and queens would hear him and praise him, and if he were a charming fellow would make a sort of favorite of him. I think he would be a charming fellow, don't you? He has a bright, handsome face."

The girl with the grey eyes turned to look down at her friend — (she was the taller of the two)—with her soft, caressing, little laugh.

"I think he would," she said; "we will imagine he would be perfectly beautiful and perfectly delightful as we *are* imagining things. It makes the story prettier."

"That is the advantage of imagining," said her friend. "One can make the story as pretty as one likes. I wonder if he has a mother in the Città Vecchia, and if he would remember her and her love when he was a great tenor? Let us imagine that he would—and imagine how proud and radiantly happy she would be. Poor little peasant woman, I hope the grandeur and the kings and queens would not frighten her."

"Think how she would feel sitting in a box at the opera—at La Scala, for instance," said the girl. "She would have had to lay aside her short petticoats and her peasant bodice, and have learned to wear a bonnet instead of a red and yellow and green handkerchief tied over her head."

"And she would have very large grand ear-rings, I am sure," went on the lady in black, with a little softly-smiling reflective air. "Giovanni would have given them to her for a present. Don't you think she would choose some of those big ancient ones we see in the curiosity shops, with queer stones in them and a great deal of turquoise? They say those have all been bought from peasants. I think she would be sure to want a pair. Diamonds would seem quite cold and plain to her, dear simple old thing. She would want turquoise and garnets and amethysts and yellow old pearls set elaborately in silver gilt."

"How real she seems," smiled the girl with the grey eyes; and then they looked at each other, and her friend smiled also.

"Well," she said, "he has a voice—and he might have a career—and it is more than probable that he has a mother—so it is easy to imagine a story for him. I wish we could do something to help to make it real. Why should he eat polenta and live like a peasant always if he has a gift? I am going to think about him, and see if—well, if there is anything to be done."

"You always want to make your stories come true, don't you?" said her companion.

The lady in black looked out far over the sunlight sapphire sea. She seemed to be thinking of something that stirred in her a sad tenderness.

"I might make him one of Leo's friends," she said, "one of those boys he helps."

"You are always thinking of Leo, I think," the girl said very gently. "He seems very near to you, dear."

"Very near," was the answer. "I could not let him seem far away. He is more real than anything else. Sometimes I think he seems even more real than Geof, who is alive and strong and happy, and always busy. A year ago Leo was alive and like him. He was so strong and bright, and so full of the things he was interested in. I can't let him go just because of that morning when his brown eyes closed so softly and his arms unclasped themselves and slipped slowly away from my neck. I must comfort myself in some way—so I try to imagine things about him too—and I try to make them seem quite real."

The girl with the grey eyes put her hand through her arm and drew it to her side with a tender pressure.

" Dear ! " she said.

Two large quiet drops slipped down her friend's cheeks, but no others followed them, and she went on speaking, with even a little smile on her lips.

" I say to myself that he has gone to a Fair Far Country," she said. " Perhaps it is because I am a very earthly person that I have to make it so real to myself. I tell myself that other mothers' sons go away to far countries to live. You know there are so many who go to foreign lands to make their fortunes. But their mothers do not feel as if they had lost them. And I know they must comfort themselves by doing things for them and reading books about the countries they have gone to. If Leo had gone to Africa, think how I should have read about Africa. As it is, I read over and over the parts of those last chapters which tell about the City, the City that has streets of pure gold, like unto clear glass. It always seemed like a beautiful fairy story, until Leo went away. And then I was so hungry for him—it seemed as if I *must* have something *real* to think of, so I began to read, and imagine. I wish there was more to read. I like to remember that 'the gates of it shall not be shut at all by day—and there is no night there.' He was so happy when he was on earth, I can't help trying to make it a place that would not seem too dazzling and strange and solemn for a boy to like. He was only such a boy, you know, and at first I could not help feeling timid and hoping that it would not overwhelm and bewilder him. I try to remember more about the green pastures and the river of crystal than about the walls of jasper and sapphire, and emerald, and the streets of gold. But somehow I love the gates made of great pearls, and always standing open."

"You do make it real, don't you, dear?" said the girl.

"I *must* make it real, I *must* do things to comfort myself and make me feel that I am not letting him go. That is why I have my fancy about helping those other boys whom I call his friends. If he had lived to be a man he might have had sorrow and pain and disappointment — he might have known temptation and have fallen into human fault. That is all over for him — he can never be touched now. Why should not I go on with the sweet *kind* things he might have done? You know there would have been many of them. He had a tender, generous heart—and in the life of a man with a heart like that there must be many good things done for others, even if there should be human weakness and sorrow too. I don't want the sweet things to go undone just because he has died. That would be as if those he might have helped had been robbed of a friend. When he was a baby I used to say, 'I want the big world to be better just because he lives.' Now I say, 'I want it to be better even that he has lived—and died.'"

"And that is why you are so interested in Giovanni? I knew it was like that, dear," with another soft pressure of the arm.

"In Giovanni—in any boy whose life might be made brighter and broader—in any boy who needs help or a friend. It might not always be money that would help them most. It might be something else. Whatever is done, it is not I who do it—it is Leo. Leo, who will never be tempted or made sad by life, but who goes on living and holding out his kind, boyish, friendly young hand to other boys who must finish their lives and bear all the burdens of them. He was spared them all. He lived a few bright, buoyant, joyous years without a shadow or a stain. Now he seems to me like

a magnificent, fair young prince in his royal city,
with his hands full of royal gifts, and his soul full
of tender yearning for those who are outside the
gates and who must toil longer in the heat of the
sun."

"And he will help Giovanni?" said her friend.
"I see that."

"He will try," was the answer.

III

THE little *salon* out of which one stepped on to
the white marble balcony was a very pretty one.
It had not been particularly pretty when the lady
in black and her friend first took possession of it.
Then it had worn the usual ungarnished air of
nearly all hotel rooms. Now it was quite bright
and gay. The curiosity shops had been levied
upon for antique brocades, for rich tenderly-faded
old vestments whose colors of a hundred or two
years ago had melted into wondrous shades, and
which were draped on the walls, and thrown over
pieces of furniture. There were many cushions
covered with squares of such brocade, there were
draperies over the doors, there were Spanish fans
and odd trifles here and there, there were studies
of peasants and the Città Vecchia, and branches of
orange trees, and olives, and eucalyptus blossom,
there were bits of Louis Quatorze silver and
china, and painted and gilded fans on the mantel ;
there were bowls and vases of jonquils and mimosa, and narcissi and violets everywhere—there
were many violets, the air was full of their breath,
and wheresoever one's eye turned it rested on the

pictured face of a boy, who watched one with shadowy velvet dark eyes. There were several pictures of him, and each one had before it a cluster of violets.

"He had always been used to seeing me wear violets," his mother said. "When he was a little fellow he used to bring me all he could find in the garden. And the first time he was in London he saw some crystallized bunches in a confectioner's in Regent Street, and he spent all his pennies to buy me some, and brought them to me for a present, with such an innocent pride. When he was ill and people sent him flowers, he used to say to his nurse: 'Give all the violets to mammie. All the violets are for her.' When he went to sleep that last day I covered him with them. In the medallion with his miniature, which I always wear, there is one shut inside with him. They mean so much more to me now."

When they were not walking or driving together she and the girl with the grey eyes used to sit in this little *salon* among the flowers and soft colors and talk of their problems and dreams and imaginings. They had a great many. Theirs was a very dear friendship. They loved and understood each other very tenderly and completely. They had the same emotions, the same fancies. There was never any danger that one could be too imaginative or subtle for the other. They had

the same tastes and sympathies and the shades in
which they varied only gave interest to their
thoughts and words.

The evening after they had met Giovanni was
mild and warm, and the windows on the balcony
were open. The lady in black lay upon a sofa
with many cushions. In the midst of their quiet
talk the strings of a guitar were touched in the
garden below. It was rather a good guitar, and
the opening bars of a song were being played.

"Some one is going to sing," said the lady in
black; "but it is not Giovanni. He is always
with the harpist."

And then they heard the singer begin his song.

"It is far from being Giovanni's voice," exclaimed Gertrude. "Poor thing, how bad it is."

Her friend raised her head to listen.

"And it is a boy's voice, too," she said; "but
it sounds all strained and cracked. Ah, how piti-
ful. He ought not to sing at all."

"It *is* strained," said Gertrude. "Poor boy, it
has been a good voice once—perhaps as good as
Giovanni's. But he has been singing too much,
and has forced it until it is broken. What a cruel
pity!"

It was a piteous enough thing to hear—the poor
voice rising from among the palms and roses below. It was so roughened, so strained and broken.

"It makes me sad," said the mother. "It sounds

so mournful rising out of the dark. Giovanni comes and sings in the morning when all the world is full of sunshine, and he seems like a happy young bird. This poor boy stands alone there in the darkness as if he knew his helplessness and did not care to be seen. I wonder if Giovanni knows him; if he knows Giovanni, and if it is not a bitter thing for him. Let us go and look down at him."

They went out on to the balcony and looked down, but they could not really see the singer. They could only imagine they saw a shadow which might after all be part of the shade behind some orange trees; but the poor hoarse voice struggled through the song to the end.

" No one opens the windows to throw him money," said the lady in black. " They don't want to hear him. I do not want to hear him—it is too sad; but I shall throw him money. He needs it more than Giovanni. Everybody gives *him* something—every one wants him. No one wants the poor other one."

They put some silver in an envelope and threw it down. The shadow seemed to move forward slowly and as if with a dragging step.

" Do you know," said the lady in black, " I have a fancy that he really does not care to be seen. Let us go back into the *salon*." And they quietly slipped away.

This was the opening of the story of "the Other."   It was a sad story and he was never more than a shadow. They always called him "the Other," and they never saw him; but they spoke of him even more than they spoke of Giovanni whom they saw three times a week.

Somehow the poor cracked voice singing in the darkness had touched them very much. It was so evident that it had been a beautiful voice once, and that only bad management and perhaps bad health had been its ruin.

"Do you know who the poor boy is who sang last night?" they asked the *concierge*.

"No, Madame," was the answer, though the *concierge* usually knew everything. "He does not come often and it is always dark. It is very bad — his singing. The people do not like it. They say it disturbs them, it is so bad."

"It is too late to save his voice now," the two friends said to each other afterwards, "but if we could do something kind for him it would be a comfort."

Only it was plain that he did not wish to be seen. He came only rarely, and always at night, and always stood in the shadow of the trees. So they could only throw him money and go back to their *salon* and talk to each other about him pityingly.

Somehow they never could hear Giovanni or

speak of him without speaking also of "the Other."

" No one but ourselves throws him money," said the lady in black, sadly, once. " Perhaps he is poor and comes just for what he gets from us. It makes it all the sadder. Think of going about from place to place singing in that dreary, piteous voice, and knowing that no one wishes to listen, and that if money is given it is only from pity or to rid one's self of the annoyance of hearing. To me it seems a sort of tragedy. It is tragic if he is a boy who feels and thinks. I cannot help hoping that he does not know Giovanni, and so cannot feel the contrast. Giovanni is so rosy and strong and plump—I feel as if ' the Other' must be thin and haggard and pale."

" He is a story to you, too," said Gertrude.

" Yes, and I cannot make it anything but a sad one."

Because it was a sad one her mind dwelt on it. She found herself wondering each day if at night the broken voice would sing in the dark. They did not hear it more than half a dozen times, and it was heard on no stated day.

" Perhaps it is wrong even to throw the money to him," she said. " It may be that it encourages him to sing ; and, perhaps, if he did not sing at all and gave his poor voice a rest it might recover itself. Do you think it might, Gertrude ?"

"I am afraid not," Gertrude answered; "I am afraid it is too far gone."

The next day they sent the *concierge* to ask Giovanni to come to their *salon* to talk to them.

He came in the afternoon, evidently feeling a little awkward, but looking rosy and pleased. He had had too much simple success and good luck to be really very shy.

It was certainly true that he was not the restless, yearning, ambitious musical genius of romance. He was a simple, well-favored, good-humored little peasant, fond of music in a primitive unimpassioned way, and appreciative of the good fortune which had given him a good voice. They found out that he had sometimes been to school, that he once had three "mentions," that he was rather tired of street singing, that he had been taught something of music by a certain Maestro Mecheri, whose business it was to train the choruses at the tiny theatre. All that he knew of his singing he had learned from Maestro Mecheri.

"Does he tell you that you have a very good voice?" asked the lady in black.

"Yes, Signora, he says it is a good voice."

"And he tells you, I dare say, that you must take care of it and not strain it at all?"

"Yes, Signora, he warns me of that."

"You see," the lady went on, leaning a little forward and smiling, "you are growing. In a short time it will change into a young man's voice; and if you force it and go on singing while it is changing you may spoil it for ever. But if you are careful it may become such a voice as— as everybody shall care to hear. Has Maestro Mecheri told you that?"

It was plain that Maestro Mecheri was not an imaginative person himself, and that he confined himself to the present and his immediate surroundings principally. The limitations of his experience were perhaps good enough under the circumstances.

"He says that I must not sing in the streets much longer," said Giovanni; "and I must live well, and not ramble about at night."

"He is quite right," said the lady in black. "Have you ever thought that you would like to choose music for a profession—to care for your voice and train it and be a musician—a singer?" She spoke with a sense of some inward uncertainty. He was so good-temperedly prosaic about it all.

He smiled and gave a little shrug of his shoulders. "I should like it," he said. "Sometimes they make fortunes, they say—those who have good voices and sing on the stage."

"Yes," said the lady in black. "A beautiful voice is a great gift and brings great fortune sometimes. When you stop singing in the street it would be a good thing for you to go to school again if you could. It would prepare you to learn other things better — to train your voice and study music more easily—if the time came when you wanted to do it. Maestro Mecheri would tell you that too."

" It is possible," said Giovanni. " He tells me oftenest I must not strain my voice and that I must not vagabond about at night. There is a boy we know of who had a fine—it was very fine—"

The lady in black and the girl with the grey eyes leaned a little more towards him and looked interested, and rather eager.

" He used to sing as I do," continued Giovanni. " Maestro Mecheri says his voice was even better than mine. People gave him a great deal of money when he sang. But he was not like me. He was not so strong, Maestro Mecheri said, and he was not steady in his temper. He was always talking about music and having fancies of what he might do when he grew up. He had been talked to by some Signore who came from America, and it had put ideas into his head. Me—" with a bright simple smile, " I have no ideas. The other—he had many, and they made him restless."

" The Other," exclaimed the lady in black, in English. And she and the girl with the grey eyes looked at each other again.

" They spoiled him," Giovanni went on. " He used to sing too much. Maestro Mecheri said he was too impatient, and he ought to have let his voice rest. He was older than I. He got a cold and began to cough, and he could not wait until it was better. He was hoarse and he was afraid he had lost his voice, and he would keep trying it to see if it had come back. But it sounded cracked and harsh. And he lost patience and began to vagabond about at night. Often he did not go to bed until two or three in the morning. Now his voice is quite gone, and Maestro Mecheri says it will not return."

" What is his name ? " asked Gertrude.

Giovanni gave his shade of a shrug again.

" I do not remember," he said. " I do not know him. Maestro Mecheri told me of him as a warning."

" There is a boy who comes and sings before the hotel at night sometimes," said the lady in black. " We have noticed that his voice has been spoiled. Perhaps that is he."

" Yes, that is possible," said Giovanni. " The *foresticri* used to like to hear him, and he went to all the hotels. They say there was a rich Signora at one hotel who was a singer herself, and had made her fortune, and she asked him into her *salon* one night and made him sing for her. And he pleased her so much that she told him he would have a wonderful life, and she gave him twenty-five francs for himself. They say," with an innocently amused air, " that she also kissed him."

" And now his voice is quite gone ? " exclaimed the lady in black.

" Maestro Mecheri says it is lost for ever. He should not have had ideas—and strained it, and become such a vagabond."

He said it quite simply, and without any air of ill-nature or severity. He seemed to be merely stating facts.

" Where does he live ? I wish you knew his name," the lady in black said.

" I think he lives somewhere in the Città Vecchia, but I do not know where. He is ill, they say, and seldom goes out now. He caught more cold. That was a bad thing for him."

He went away soon afterwards. They had learned where his mother lived, and that Maestro Mecheri might be found and talked to. They had not made any promises, or suggested to him the possibility of their having plans. He went off with a present of money in his pocket and smiles on his good-looking face. A few minutes before he went, as he was being shown a book of Tuscan songs, he stood near a table which held one of the pictures of the boy with the shadowy, dark eyes.

" Is this the Signorino who sings Italian, and is in America ? " he asked.

The lady in black took up another picture and passed it to him.

" No," she said gently, " this is the one who is in America."

This boy wore a lace-ruffled fancy dress, and had a brilliantly happy young face and laughing eyes. He leaned carelessly against a carven cabinet, and looked out at the beholders as if mere boyish life itself was a delightful thing. Giovanni regarded him with interest. It was evident to him that this Signorino had been born to good fortune. He was smiling himself as he laid it down.

" And this other," he said, looking at the first picture. " Does he also sing—and is he in America ? "

The boy in the picture—his noble young face turned slightly over his shoulder — seemed to meet the young peasant's eyes with a soft, questioning glance. For the moment it was as if they two looked at each other almost as they might have done if they had stood face to face.

" This one," said Giovanni, after a moment's silence. " Is he the brother of the other Signorino—and where is he ? "

The girl with the grey eyes laid her hand softly on his shoulder and spoke in a low voice, even softer than her touch.

" This one," she said, " he died three months ago."

IV

Brigita climbed slowly up the steep narrow
streets of the Città Vecchia—the streets which
were so narrow as to be mere passages between the old, old houses, protected against the
ruin of possible earthquakes by the many archways thrown across from wall to wall. It was
these old houses, and narrow, passage-like steep
streets and unexpected archways which gave the
Città Vecchia—which means simply the old city—
its picturesqueness, and made the *foresticri* climb up
to see it so often and make sketches of corners of
it. It seemed a marvellous old place to the *forestieri;* and during the winter season, when the
hotels and villas were filled with them, the peasants in the Old City became quite used to seeing
groups of two or three well-dressed people rambling about, stopping to look up dark narrow
stone stairways, or tiny iron-barred windows, or
delighting themselves with a tumble-down wall or
a crumbling arch with green weeds sprouting out
of its stones, high in the air. The *foresticri* had
these queer ways. They who were rich, and lived
in the grand hotels and white villas, and wore

wonderful garments, would stop and watch a serious mule or donkey laden with fagots or sacks of olive, stumbling honestly up the hill-side streets, its burden almost touching the walls on each side, and they would look at it as if it were a wonder, and as if the peasant-woman walking beside it with her weather-worn, dark face, framed with a red or yellow and green handkerchief tied over her black hair and under her chin, as if she were a wonder too. And sometimes they had been known to make sketches of both—as if there were not real and grand pictures of Madonnas, and saints, and angels in the fine picture galleries of the great cities they were always rambling about the world to visit. The peasants thought that all this came about because they had nothing to do, and were so idle that it made them childish.

Brigita—who was Giovanni's mother—did not suspect for a moment that she was picturesque. She did not know what picturesque meant. She knew the young men had called her a pretty girl years ago, before she had married Cola and had had children and worked so hard. Then she had been plump and had had laughing white teeth and bright eyes, and there had been red on her brown cheeks and a curl in her thick hair. But now she considered herself an old woman, though she was not one as the *foresticri* counted years. She had worked in the house, among the children and the

beasts, she had worked at the olive harvest and
the grape gathering, and had done all sorts of
things on the bit of land Cola rented in the campagna, and she had grown sinewy, and there were
lines on her face, and her black hair was always
more or less rough under the red or yellow and
green handkerchief tied over it. She had never
owned a bonnet. It would have troubled her
almost as much as a crown. It was only the
forestieri—the signoras—who wore little things
made of silk and lace and feathers and flowers.

And if she did not know that she was a picturesque object herself, how much less did she suspect that her donkey clambering by her side with
a burden of fodder twice as large as himself, was
a sort of picture also. He was a little shaggy,
gray, patient-faced beast, with soft, furry long ears
and long black eyelashes, and his grave little face
and slow toiling steps and big load were exactly
the things to put in a sketch of the narrow steep
streets with the ancient irregular houses on either
side of them, and the unexpected arches sprung
into straggling weed growth.

Brigita had been to the campagna to help Cola
with the olive gathering. Giovanni, though he
was her eldest son and of working age, had not
been with them, because they had found out that
he could be more useful to them if he were allowed
to use his time and strength in another way. His

singing was a good thing for them, and Maestro Mecheri had said it was better that he should not be put to labor that would tire him, because it was not good for his voice. And it did not matter so that he brought in help one way or another, and upon the whole his voice brought in much more than his labor in the fields or vineyards would have done.

When she had climbed up the street to her own door and unloaded the donkey and driven him into his rough stable with the iron-barred windows, she gave him some food and mounted the steep, dark stone stairway which took to the rooms where she lived.

When she opened the door and entered the living room a wiry little elderly man rose from a chair at her entrance.

"Good day, Brigita," he said. "I have been waiting for you."

It was Maestro Mecheri.

"Good day, Maestro," she answered. "I have been at work at the olive gathering with Cola. There is quite a good crop, but the olives are small. There has not been enough rain."

"That is true," answered Maestro Mecheri. "We have needed rain for many weeks. I have come to talk with you about Giovanni."

"Has anything gone wrong with him?" she asked.

"No," said Maestro Mecheri, "he has good luck, that *ragazzo*. He has a fine voice and is strong, and not troubled with ideas. And he is good-looking. Often I believe money is given as much to his merry eyes and white teeth as to his singing. The *foresticri* like his cheerful, handsome face. It is good luck to be born looking like that. It has possibly made his fortune for him."

"In what way, Santa Maria!" exclaimed Brigita.

"The *foresticri* have ways of their own," said the Maestro. "There are two Signore who have heard him sing and have taken a fancy to him."

"Yes," Brigita interrupted, "they sent the *concierge* of their hotel to tell him to come to their *salon* the other day. Giovanni told me about it. It was all hung with old brocades and pictures and fans, such as one sees in the shops for antiquities, and it was filled with flowers, and there were many pictures of a boy who is dead. His mother was the one who sent the *concierge* to Giovanni."

"Yes," said Maestro Mecheri, "that is it—and that is the point. That is why I say they have ways of their own, the *foresticri*. Most people when a child dies—if they are rich—bury him finely and have masses said and hang black and white bead wreaths on his tomb. They are very handsome, those bead wreaths with 'mio figlio,' or 'mia madre,' and other sentiments upon them. I have even seen a little weeping willow made of green beads bending over a headstone. There are beautiful ornaments for the dead made of beads. And this signora must be rich, but she seems to have queer ideas; she did not explain them much to me, but I gathered some of her fancies from some few things she said. It seems as if she were not content that the boy's life should be ended on earth and continue only in Paradise. She has a strange wish that he should seem still to live on earth and do things for other boys. It is singular, but it is a good thing for Giovanni. She came to see me about him."

Brigita made a gesture of amazement. Her eyes had been wide open before; now her mouth opened.

"Yes," continued the Maestro, scratching his grizzled, curling poll; "she has a wish that this boy of hers—who is in Paradise—should help Giovanni. She did not say it exactly, but I could see she had some fancy—I guessed it from her face, and from her voice which trembled when she spoke. I am not a dull fellow."

"What does she want to do?" said Brigita. "It makes one feel strange—such an idea, I am not sure I like it. It might bring ill-fortune—like the evil eye—to have a person who is dead watching over one."

Maestro Mecheri shrugged his shoulders.

"That is stupid," he said. "It is the idea of a peasant." He knew that Brigita was a peasant and quite a common and ordinary one, and he who was a professional person connected with the theatre did not shrink from speaking his mind to her. "It is a good thing for Giovanni, and her plans are sensible in spite of her fancies. She says that he has a voice which might bring him fame and fortune, if he does not strain it by singing too long, and if it is trained afterwards. She says that out of the fortune of her son she will pay you a sum which will make it possible for you and Cola to afford to let him stop singing in the street, and he shall go to school for a year or so, until his voice is changed. I am to watch over him and let her know when it will be safe to begin training him. And I am in the meantime to teach him all I know about music, that it may help him when he can begin practising."

"It is like a romance," said Brigita, staring. "They have ideas—the *forestieri*. It is well they have money also."

Maestro Mecheri rubbed his chin and looked at her with a superior scrutiny. It was of course natural that a peasant woman should not understand all this might mean.

"It may make a rich man of him," he said. "If his voice is a very fine one—as I think it will be

—he may make a great fortune. He may sing in great cities—perhaps before the king—and the impressarios will pay immense sums every night. It was so with Mario, it is so with Patti. There is nothing so valuable as a voice all the world wants to hear."

Brigita laughed a little.

"One cannot bring one's mind all at once to thinking that of one's own child," she said. "It would be queer enough to think of Giovanni singing before the king!"

"If he has good fortune," said Maestro Mecheri, "that may all come in time. The Signora wished me to see you and Cola and explain to you and ask you if you were willing. She is going away soon herself and wishes it arranged."

Brigita laughed a little vaguely again.

"You must come and see Cola," she said.

"You will not be such imbeciles as to refuse?" said the Maestro.

"What one has, one has," she answered, "and one cannot be sure of what his voice will be when he is a young man. But as she will give something to make up to us for losing his work now, I do not think Cola will care. And as for me—it is all the same so that one has something in one's hand."

"He could not sing more than a year," said the Maestro. "You know how the other boy's voice

was lost and how he broke down. His was magnificent," with another rub at his grizzled curls,
and a queer look and tone of regret. "It was
magnificent. He would have sung before the
king—it could not have been otherwise. It was
a great misfortune for him."

"You mean the son of Lisa?" said Brigita.
"He died last night, and she is almost mad, they
say."

Maestro Mecheri's look of regret took on a
sudden spasmodic deepening.

"Did he?" he said. "*Poverino! Poverino!*"

"He has been dying for months," said Brigita,
"but she would not believe it. He coughed until
he was worn to a skeleton."

"Ah!" sighed Maestro Mecheri. "And he
might have sung before kings! It was a wonderful voice."

"But he is dead," said Brigita, unemotionally.
"He died last night."

V

THE lady in black and her friend had always been very fond of the Città Vecchia. They often climbed up the steep hillside streets and visited the most unique corners of it. They knew the narrowest passages, the archways, and dark little stone stairways; the queer barred windows through which one could look into the darkness and see a sheep or two, or a donkey, or a calf. They knew the fountains where water was drawn and the big one where the women stood around the square stone basin and washed their clothes, talking and laughing together. They knew the white church at the top of the highest point, the Madonna della Costa, where the peasants went to Mass, and where there were so many queer votive pictures — small, violently colored and strangely designed things representing the scene of some catastrophe from which the victim had been rescued by some patron saint. These were always interesting to examine, as each one told its story. There were pictures of storms at sea with fisher boats apparently about to be engulfed, there were pictures of runaway

horses on the point of dashing some one to pieces,
there were others of lightning striking, of suffer-
ers from dangerous illness, from casualties of all
kinds, and generally in some corner was depicted
the figure of the Saint or Madonna descending
from Paradise to interpose the sacred protection
between the victim and impending death. Each
one had been given in commemoration and grati-
tude. They were simple and primitive beyond
description, but the faith they showed was a
touching thing.

" Only," the girl's friend used to say to her, " I
should like to know who the artist is who does
them. They are so wonderful. Perhaps there is
an artist among the peasants in the Città Vecchia
who does them all, and is quite celebrated in his
way."

During the last days the two friends spent in
San Remo they went two or three times to the
old city.

One beautiful afternoon they turned into the
climbing streets after leaving their favorite flower
shop, loaded with white narcissus and hyacinths,
gold-yellow daffodils, and scarlet and pink anemones. They climbed to Brigita's house and up
her dark little stone stairway to pay her a visit.

Brigita looked with open curiosity at the Signora, whose mass of flowers looked so bright
against her black dress and pale face.

But there was nothing eccentric or curious about her. She was very quiet and civil, and had a low voice, and eyes which seemed to have wept a great deal.

" She has wept for the boy who is in Paradise," Brigita thought. "*Poverina!* but he is better there, after all—though it is true he was a Signorine."

The visit was not a long one. It was all settled about Giovanni by this time. Cola had given his consent and the rest had been easily arranged. The *foresticri*, it seemed, did not hesitate about parting with their money when they had decided to do so. Giovanni had the chance to be a singer if he chose to work and his voice turned out well.

Among other things the Signora had given Brigita a new dress and bright head handkerchief. The handkerchief was quite wonderful and the dress was one that would last for years.

" But when Giovanni is a great tenor," said the Signora, smiling, "you will have more dresses than one."

Brigita smiled also, good-humoredly.

" That is a long time to look forward to," she said ; " who knows what will happen ? "

" I hope what happens will make you both happy," the Signora said.

" Giovanni," said Brigita, " he will, of course,

be happy if he becomes well-to-do; and, for the matter of that, so shall I."

She was standing near the window when she said this, and she looked out and shrugged her shoulders pityingly.

"Ah, there goes one who is not happy," she said; "it is that poor Lisa, whose boy died."

"Poor woman!" exclaimed the Signora, drawing near; "when did she lose him?"

"Only two weeks ago," Brigita answered. "And it seems as if she would go after him. He used to sing, too, like Giovanni, and he lost his voice and caught cold, and fell ill and coughed himself to death. Before he was too ill to leave his bed, he used to drag himself to the terrace below the church and sit on the low wall and stare down into the olive vineyards and over the sea to the point where one can see the other church — the Madonna della Guardia. He was very wretched after his voice was gone. It seemed as if he did not care to live. And now his mother goes and leans on that wall every afternoon when her work is done, and stares, as he used to, at the church, and the olives, and the sea, only that she is always crying. They say she is crying herself blind. Her man died young; she had nothing but the boy."

The girl with the grey eyes approached her friend and put a light, loving hand on her shoulder.

"It is very sad," she said.

"It is the story of 'the Other,'" the lady in black answered. "I knew it must be sad; I felt it in my heart."

4

WHEN they found themselves out in the street a little later, it was as if involuntarily they turned towards the steps which led to the church of Madonna della Costa. Just below the inclined paved steps leading to it was the terrace with the low wall, against which one could lean and look down the almost precipitous hillside on to the olive vineyards and the shallow stream. By turning one's gaze to the right, one swept across olives and villas and palms to the curve of the shore, from which rose the hill where the white little church of Madonna della Guardia kept watch over the blue sea and those who braved its dangers—if there could ever lurk dangers in the softly rippling lake-like calm.

It was a lovely point to look out from, this low wall high up in the "old city," which was so tiny that it was more like a precipitous, huddled village than a town, though it was always called the "Città Vecchia."

As the friends drew near this point, they saw the figure of a peasant woman leaning with arms folded on the grassy stone ledge before her. She

was not only poorly, but carelessly dressed. One
imagined that she had felt that it was of no con-
sequence to herself or to others if her bodice was
ill-fastened, her crinkly black hair unkempt, and
her head handkerchief ill-tied and awry.

She was staring straight before her at the hills
and the sea, and, seemingly, scarcely noticing the
words of another woman who stood by her with
a bundle of fagots on her head and her hand on
her hip.

But the two *forestieri* heard what this woman
was saying in a well-meaning but commonplace
tone.

" *Patienza*, Lisa, *patienza !* " she said. " Of what
good is all this ? Sorrow is natural enough when
one's child dies, if one has not so many that one
can be spared because one feels that it will be
better cared for. But to go mad with grief and
weep one's eyes away when one has no one left
to be eyes and hands for one—nothing but harm
can come of it. And it cannot be denied that he
could never have been happy again—Pasquale !
He had lost his voice for good, and could not
turn to anything else because he was always
mourning and wretched. It is not as if he had
kept his health and his voice as well, and had been
a healthy, handsome fellow like Giovanni, whom
they say some rich *forestieri* have taken a fancy to
and are going to make into a grand singer."

Lisa turned her face upon the speaker. Her tear-inflamed eyes seemed suddenly to glare a little like a panther's.

"Hush!" she said. "I know about that; you may be sure enough some one told me. You may be sure that now is the time—now that he is dead—dead—like that—that I shall hear of some other—some other—"

She choked and dropped her head in her hands. Her thin breast heaved and struggled as if it were imprisoning some fierce swelling thing which struggled to get out.

"Go," she said. "I wish you no ill—but carry your fagots home. You mean well, but I want to stand here alone."

The peasant woman stared at her a second with a questioning face, and then she shrugged her shoulders and went away, turning into the sloping street near by.

The lady in black was breathing quickly.

"It is the mother of 'the Other,'" she whispered to her friend. "I can understand. She is like me—only that my boy was not tired of his life. Perhaps two women like us will know what to say to each other."

The girl's grey eyes had tears in them.

"Yes," she said—"yes, dear, but she will not know that I can understand, too; she will only think that I am a Signorina and one of the

SHE PUT OUT HER HAND AND LAID IT ON THE PEASANT'S ARM

foresticri, and she won't want me. I will slip away."

It was a curious thing which happened when the lady in black drew quietly near to the peasant. Her consoler having left her, the woman had covered her worn face—almost clutched it—with her hands, and the straining, swelling wild thing heaving her breast had broken its bounds and was shaking her with tearing sobs.

It was an awful thing. Only mothers sob like that—mothers who have looked into a yawning grave where beautiful young hope and exultant buoyancy and strength lie still—still and alone.

The other mother felt the wild thing swelling in her own breast, and tearing it. Great drops rushed up and swept down her face, and she put out her hand and laid it on the peasant's arm.

" I—know you cannot help it," she said brokenly.

They were the first simple words that came to her. Somehow it seemed merely human that there should be at that moment no barrier between them. They were not Signora and peasant—*forestiere* and Italian woman of the people, they were only two mothers who had lost the blood of their hearts.

The woman raised her poor face, wet, lined, desperate.

Their eyes looked into each other.

The other mother's face was wet, too, and suddenly she, too, leaned against the wall.

"Your boy died," she said. "Mine is dead, too."

"Yes," said Lisa, hoarsely, and looking at the pale face and black draperies. "I have heard them speak of you. But you—you are a rich Signora—and he, your son, he wanted nothing." And she bowed her head again.

"He—he wanted *life*," whispered the lady in black; "and I could not give it him!" She pressed her hand on her breast. "I could not buy it, or beg it, or search for it on my hands and knees, or work for it like a servant, as if I had never been a lady at all. *No one* could sell it or give it to me—no one in all the great, powerful, wonderful world where the wise men know so much. I had always given him everything else; he thought I could give him anything — but I could not give him that; and he was so young, and it seemed so beautiful to him, and he *wanted* it!" And she bowed her head, too.

"Pasquale"—said Lisa—"my boy did not want it."

"Try—try to be comforted that he was not forced to bear it," said the other. "But, ah! poor woman! God help you, if he did not want it."

"He wanted it once," cried the peasant; "he

loved it three years ago, two years ago. It was all the voice — the beautiful silver voice that broke his heart—that was false and deserted him, that tricked him and left him to die."

"Poor boy! Poor boy!" wept the woman near her. And the peasant knew that the tears were for the young dead she had never seen.

"He always sang," she went on; "when he was a tiny thing with round cheeks and big, black eyes—so pretty that the *foresticri* stared at him and gave him *soldi* for his good looks and his long eye-lashes—even then he could sing. He used to try and make sounds like the birds, and if he heard an air in the street he would try to repeat it, and then clasp his little hands and laugh for pleasure when he had made it right. And I was proud of it, and boasted of him to the neighbors, and made him sing for them. He was like a little bird; he put his head on one side like one when he sat on my knee and sang looking from under his lashes. They were as long as that," measuring on her fingers, " and he had curls like a Gesu Bambino, and soft cheeks and strange eyes which seemed always to be listening for music in the air, such as we could not hear. And I was proud and let him sing. I ought to have put my hand over his little red mouth and killed it then—then; that voice of silver and gold that was such a traitor and a false friend."

"But you loved it and were happy," said her hearer. "I know; I have one boy left. He sings."

"The saints give to him that it may not end in grief," said Lisa. "We were poor peasants, poor enough, when he was old enough to go into the streets; it was a fine thing for us that he could go and sing. He was so handsome, and his voice was such a wonder that the *foresticri* liked him. They gave him money and were always praising and petting him. There was no other boy who lived like him. It was almost as if he had been a real Signorine, though he lived here in the Città Vecchia. If he did not sing one day before a hotel or a villa, the next day they would ask why he did not come. If he had been only like other boys and cared for nothing but the praise and the money, it would have been all right. But he was not like that. He had strange feelings about his music, and he was always finding something to read about singing and great singers. I loved him and he loved me, and I listened with all my heart when he talked, but I did not quite understand. He knew I did not, but still he loved me, and always told his thoughts to me. He loved his voice, it was his treasure, and he wanted his life to be all music. He was willing to work all day and all night if he might sing well in the end. And they told him — the *foresticri*, who knew

about voices, and Maestro Mecheri — that he
might some day be a great singer—a great one!"

"He might have been," said the listener.
"Yes, I know that is true. He might have been
and—" She hesitated a moment with parted
lips; a strange light of thought seemed to leap
into her eyes, and rest there, though she did not
finish.

"He used to come here and lean against the
wall at sunset," said Lisa. "He would look out
over the sea to the Madonna della Guardia, and
it would seem as if he were in a dream. When
he came in to eat it would seem as if he had just
wakened with a smile on his lips. It was then
that he was seeing his visions of what he would
do when he was a young man, and the whole
world loved him because his voice was of silver
and gold."

Her voice fell, and she remained silent a moment, resting her forehead on her hand. Then
she began again :

"I do not know how it first changed," she said;
"Maestro Mecheri thought that he was not really
strong, though he looked so, and he caught cold,
and sang when he should not. One day he came
in to me with a strange look on his face. He told
me that he had tried to sing, but he could not.
His voice had sounded as if it were the voice of
another. He tried to be patient at first. He

waited two days, and then went out again. But he could not make the right sounds. It was like that many times—then he tried to rest, and still it seemed to do no good. Maestro Mecheri said he did not wait long enough, and perhaps his voice had already begun to change, or perhaps it was that his malady had even then struck him. One night when I came in I found him sitting alone. His face was white, and his forehead was damp with sweat. He was hoarse when he spoke. He said, 'I cannot sing, I cannot sing; I have lost it.' I tried to console him, but it seemed as if he could not hear what I was saying. He had been to one of the villas where the people had always praised him, and they had not opened the window, or sent him money. And as he had been going away wondering and heavy-hearted, a servant had seen him, and said, 'Was it you singing? No one knew it was you. They thought it was a stranger. It did not sound like your voice. What is wrong?'

"After that it seemed as if he grew desperate. In spite of his hoarseness he would try to sing alone. He would shut himself up, and exercise his voice. He said that if he worked steadily it might come back. He began to cough, and became thin, and he could not sleep at night, but he could not give up.

"Once, when he was exercising, I heard suddenly that he had stopped, and I went quietly and stole a glance at him through the door. He was lying upon the floor weeping with heavy sobs. I dared not speak to him. He was my son, and he loved me, but there were times when I felt he was far beyond me in some strange way, and I was only a peasant woman. But he loved me, he loved me. My heart was so warm to him, and so faithful. *Scusi*, Signora, I am telling you a long story."

" Tell it to me, tell it," said the lady in black; " it will ease your heart to speak. Sometimes one wishes to be quite silent, one cannot speak at all, but sometimes one must go over it all again, one cannot help it. Tell it all to me."

" Yes, it is so," said the peasant woman; " but there are so few one can speak to."

" We have both felt the same suffering," said the lady in black.

" To be a mother who loves must be the same always," said Lisa. " I have knelt before the Madonna in the church there, feeling that she must understand. She was like us after all. She had held her Son in her arms, and she stood by and saw him die, and could not help him." And she made the sign of the cross.

" I used to ask myself if she looked on," she went on—" if she looked down at the Città Vecchia in those months that came after. Surely the

Calvary was not more terrible. They were so long, so long."

"And so short," the other mother said, in a voice like a cry. And she caught the peasant woman's hand. "I know it all, they were so long, and so short."

"Yes. Yes. Did yours die so?"

"Yes."

"Mine wasted and coughed, and his eyes grew large and hollow, and his hair was damp, and he was weaker every day; but always he would try, with his poor voice, to sing, and always it grew hoarser and feebler, and more cracked—his gold and silver voice. And when he heard it he would let his damp forehead fall on his hand, and large tears would roll down his cheeks. He ceased early to try and sing before the villas and hotels in the daylight. He used to steal out at night and try in the darkness. He did not wish to be seen; but no one gave him anything; they had all forgotten him, and once a *concierge* came out to tell him he must go away, that he disturbed the guests. In that hotel they had once made him their favorite. It does not take long for the happy rich ones to quite forget. It was terrible to him to find out that he had been so quickly forgotten. That night, after the *concierge* came out to tell him to go away, he did not sleep at all. His pillow was wet in the morning, and it was not only

with the dampness of his hair, but with tears.
His eyes had great shadows under them, and he
was exhausted. Some nights he used to wander
about until it was long past midnight. Those
who did not know him said he had got into a bad
way, and was a vagabond. But I knew that it
was not so.

"One night—it was the last time he tried to sing
at all—he came in with something in his hand,
and sat and stared at it. Mother of God! he
looked like a ghost—a lost spirit—a condemned
soul!

"'There are some people at the Grand Hôtel
des Anglais,' he said; 'they are *forestieri*, two Signore. Once or twice they have thrown out money
to me. They are generous. I suppose they are
rich. I know why they throw it to me, it is because they pity me—they pity me. They hear
how bad it is, how broken and hideous. They
know I have lost it, and they are sorry. To-night
they threw me this from their balcony.' And he
held out his wasted, trembling hand with a piece
of silver in it. 'Once they would have given it
from pleasure. That is over. It is gone! I shall
never sing again!'

"He kept the piece of silver, because he said it
reminded him of the time when such things fell
to him from so many balconies and windows, and
this was the last he should ever have."

She sobbed a little, and rubbed her eyes with the end of her handkerchief.

"After that he only lay in his bed. He coughed and burned with fever, but I would not believe that it was all over. He had been such a beauty, and had sung so well a year before, and he was so young—only a boy—Mother of God! only fifteen years old!

"One night—it is not a month ago—he slept restlessly and at last he began to sing in a weak, harsh voice, panting and broken; it was *Addio bella Napoli* he began, but the strange broken sound wakened him. He started and stared at me as if it were I whose voice he had heard.

"'Who sang?' he whispered; 'who sang?' But a moment later he lifted his head from the pillow a little, as if he were listening. It was very strange; he was as white as snow, but he faintly smiled. His eyes did not see me, he—he was listening to something I could not hear!

"'Ah! that is better,' he said softly, and while he seemed to listen a breath of something seemed to pass across his face, and make it quite still, even the smile, and his parted lips and open eyes.

"I held my own breath for a second. And then his head sank on the pillow, and his eyes closed."

Is there anyone who can say it was a strange

thing that the gloved hand and the bare rough one caught and clung to each other, and that two women sobbed as they leaned upon the Città Vecchia's old gray wall, and felt their hearts beat against its stoniness!

5

VII

MANY things happen during ten years, and yet
at the end of them it seems as though somehow
after all the time had flown very quickly! Young
things have grown to manhood, fortunes and
reputations have been made, so many structures
have been built up stone by stone, or have fallen
into dust and been forgotten. People have grown
happy or sad, good or bad; lives have begun, and
lives have ended. And yet one says, with sudden
wonder, "Can it be ten years since then—really
ten years?"

During the ten years after the two mothers
stood by the wall on the steep of the Città Vecchia, many things had come to pass in the queer
old town which had always seemed to be crumbling.

The mother who was one of the *foresticri* had
been Lisa's friend before she had gone away herself. The two had understood each other. Lisa
had been enabled to live and work quietly in her
old house without fear of suffering from poverty.
She had not wanted much, and she had a friend
who would not desert her, though she was far

away. Over the mound where her boy lay, there
was a slender white cross, and upon the mound
many a flower grew. On the cross the peasant
woman used to hang garlands. On the coast of
the Mediterranean one may afford flowers.

There were things the stranger mother had
said in their talks together, which Lisa had taken
to her heart and always remembered. They were
things of which she did not speak much to others,
but her thoughts dwelt on them with strange
comfort when her day's work was over, and she
used to go and lean upon the low wall and look
towards the hill where the Madonna della Guardia watched over the sapphire sea.

" In Paradise," she used to whisper to herself.
" They say that even those who have not sung on
earth have voices given to them. What joy he
would feel when it all came back to him more
golden and clear than ever! How the saints
would listen to him—and the Madonna herself.
Surely she would smile and keep him near her,
because he had suffered so on earth! And the
signorino—who was a boy too, and had so many
boy friends on earth—perhaps—they surely must
have known each other because their mothers have
wept together. But he would sing again — he
would sing again!"

As the years went by there were many interesting stories of Giovanni. It was told in the Città

Vecchia that his voice had become a wonder, and
that he was becoming famous among the masters
who trained voices, and great things were prophesied of him. He was strong and well grown
and handsome as a picture, it was said. He had
sent a photograph of himself to Brigita and Cola,
and they were by no means averse to showing it to
their acquaintances and repeating what had been
said by the people who knew what voices were.

And then came the time when he sang for the
first time in an opera. To the Città Vecchia it
seemed like a fairy story. He had sung in a
great theatre filled with grand people and lights
and jewels—little Giovanni who had sung in the
streets, and been more than proud to bring home
a few francs. There had been wonderful scenery
on the stage—places as fine as the king's palace,
and Giovanni had moved about acting and singing as if he had been used to such things always.
And the people had been wild with joy, and had
applauded and risen in their seats and thrown
flowers at his feet, and called aloud his name.

And from that time his life was more like a
fairy story every day. It was the great excitement of the Città Vecchia, and Brigita and Cola
were a hero and heroine. They need not work
at all, they were quite rich, at least Giovanni,
who was a good fellow after all, in the midst of
his grandeur, sent them plenty of money for all

their simple wants. It was delightful to go and sit with them just to hear their stories and discover how grand the world was. Brigita and Cola always had plenty of visitors after Giovanni's career began.

And one evening those who dropped in to chat and drink a little wine comfortably found them wearing an air at once reverential and triumphant. They had just had a new letter from Giovanni, who was in Rome.

"To-night," Brigita announced almost breathlessly—"this very night he is to sing before the queen and the king! They have asked it—and all the Court will be there to hear."

.   .   .   .   .   .

It was true that on this night his audience was a very magnificent one; and that the Royal box was filled. The queen and king had come to hear this wonderful new young singer, who had risen like a star, and who had once been only a little street-singing peasant.

And because the queen and king had come the Court had followed, and the house was a splendid spectacle. There were beautiful women and rich dresses, glittering jewels and flowers and soft colors and perfumes everywhere. And everyone was talking of the marvellous young tenor and the great fame which had come to him, and the great fortune which his future held.

In one of the boxes were a lady and a young
man who were evidently not Romans, but their
interest seemed almost greater than that of the
rest of the audience. It seemed an interest a
little different from the universal one. They
were mother and son. The mother wore soft,
black draperies, and her blonde hair was pow-
dered with silver threads. The son was a graceful, happy-eyed young fellow, with a bright face
and laughing eyes. He leaned forward with a
boyish smile of pleasure.

"What a house!" he said. "What a splendid
house! I am so glad! How lovely the queen
looks to - night! The king seems in a cheerful
mood, too. They are sure to be pleased ; of
course they must be! Everything goes well for
him. What a change for a little peasant! I wish
I had seen him when he sang under your window,
and thought the francs you threw him were a
fortune! It was just after—"

He stopped and put out his warm young hand
and touched his mother's.

"You were very sad then, dear," he said.
"But out of that all Giovanni's good fortune
has come. How strange it is! If you had not
gone there, he might have sung in the streets
until he had spoiled his voice. Then he would
have had to live the life of a common peasant.
If you had not made his first step for him,

IN ONE OF THE BOXES

he might never have been able to make the others."

His mother sat a little in the shadow of the curtain and looked at the brilliantly lighted stage. She smiled a soft, vague smile.

" I wonder if he ever remembers that it was not really I who did it, but a boy like himself whom he never saw. It was Leo who was his friend."

It was a splendid, wondrous night for the young tenor. Whatsoever the triumphs that his life might bring him in the future, there would never be one which seemed quite so joyous and magnificent as this hour, when young and full of exultant spirit he poured forth his song before the brilliant house, while the king and queen applauded him with delight—the king and queen in the marvellous storied capital of his own country.

He was a beautiful young fellow of a dark-eyed simple stalwart type. He had evidently lived joyously and without pain or despondency. There were no shadows of past young suffering in his well-outlined happy face. His temperament had saved him all that. His black hair curled crisp and close over an unmarked forehead, his brown eyes had the golden clearness one sees in the eyes of some fine young animal, he had a glowing olive skin, and a body which was full of grace and strength. When he opened his fresh red lips the notes that poured forth were golden sweet.

Those who listened found it a pleasure merely to look at his joyous youth and beauty. As the scenes of the opera succeeded each other, their enthusiasm grew. The queen leaned forward smiling, the applause grew deafening. They called him out again and again, and yet again, and he came palpitating and bowing, and smiling with joy. At the end of the last act the house was throbbing with delight. Flowers rained upon him, and were so heaped about his feet that he could not remove them unaided.

The lady in black had been holding on her knee a large bunch of deep purple violets. She bent forward and threw them to him herself. He saw her, and, raising them from the showers of more brilliant color, bowed low with a radiant look.

.   .   .   .   .   .

As they rose to leave their box, the young fellow with the bright face was filled with exultant excitement.

"How perfect it all has been!" he said as he folded his mother's wrap about her. "How perfect! He could not have had a greater triumph. How happy he must be! How glorious it is to think of it! He must feel that earth can scarcely hold more."

He stopped a moment and looked down at his

mother's face. Her eyes were wet, but they were filled with a shining smile which was strangely happy. He took her hand and drew it through his arm, pressing it lovingly against his side.

"You are thinking of something, dear," he said ; " what is it ?"

She met his young eyes, her own glowing even more radiantly.

" Why," she said, " we understand each other's thoughts so well that it will not seem strangely fanciful to you. I am thinking of ' the Other.' You know how sad it was, that story of his. And just now as I saw all the flowers and the jewel-like lights, and heard the roar of applause, and glanced at the king, I thought all at once of ' the Other.' Giovanni has gained all the earth can give, but ' the Other ' has been all these years in the golden city with the open gates of pearl ! Who knows, who can know what his life has been ? He has sung too, and the King has heard him. Perhaps there was stillness through the great fair wondrous spaces while all listened. Of the two—Giovanni and ' the Other '—which of them to-night, which of them—?" And her voice fell into soft silence.

And we who know only the life of earth with all its incompleteness and longings unfulfilled, whisper with bated breath, " Which of them ? Ah ! which—Giovanni, or ' the Other ' ?"

"ILLUSTRISSIMO SIGNOR BÉBÉ"

"ILLUSTRISSIMO SIGNOR BÉBÉ"

"ILLUSTRISSIMO SIGNOR BÉBÉ"

TO begin with, I never saw him. At least I never saw anything of him but some photographs. And yet in all my gallery of children who have made stories, there is no little figure more distinct to me or more full of intense juvenile character than that of Illustrissimo Signor Bébé. I called him this because he was such an all-powerful and distinguished little person, and because, being an Italian, if he had been grown-up, instead of five years old, his letters would have been addressed, according to polite custom, Illustrissimo Signor, etc. His real name was Luigi Roberto, but no one ever called him so. He was always addressed and spoken of as Bébé, and so, after hearing innumerable delightful stories of him in which he always figured as the most magnificent autocrat and invariably managed to have his own way, I fell into the habit of speaking of him as " Illustrissimo Signor Bébé."

There is a little room in my house in London which has flowery walls and hangings, lounging chairs, and fanciful light bits of furniture. One of these bits of furniture is a fantastic little double-shelved table, with a chair, equally light and fantastic, attached. I do not know why the chair is part of the table, as it is placed sideways and nobody could sit in it and write on the table, and, in fact, the table is not made to write on at all. It is too light and small. It is made only to hold books or trifling ornaments, and this table is dedicated to Illustrissimo Signor Bébé.

In the first place there is a photograph upon a small easel. It is the picture of a most beautiful little boy of about four years old, and he seems to be far from pleased with the circumstances with which he finds himself surrounded. In fact he looks distinctly pouting, but as charming as a disgusted and too-much-photographed baby can be.

The truth was, I believe, that being an infant professional beauty he had been photographed to the verge of distraction and the limit of endurance, and finally had clutched his big sailor hat, clasped his arms over the back of the chair, and rested his curl-laden head upon them, looking out under his eye-lashes and pouting at all the world—his mamma, the photographer whom he regarded as a troublesome idiot, the little bird who would not fly out of the camera when he waited for him, and his mamma's friend and his own adorer and slave, the young lady who had

used all sorts of devices to make him sit up and
look good-tempered.

He did not feel good-tempered, he was an in-
jured and bored person, and he did not intend
to look as if he was pleased when he was really
bored to death with the imbecilities of these
people. So he put his head on his arm and
dangled his legs, and the photographer hurriedly
took the prettiest picture Illustrissimo Signor
Bébé had ever had. Nothing could have been
prettier—the tumbling mass of long curls falling
over his shoulder and shading his round cheek,
his rebellious little face, his plump mutinous legs,
which looked as if they were ready to kick, his
protesting dark eyes, and the indignant pose of
the arms, and the sailor hat scornfully held, made
not only a photograph, but a picture which told
its own story.

I should have quite adored it, even if I had not
heard all these stories about Illustrissimo Signor
Bébé and kept pace with his record, as it were,
during a whole Florentine winter, but knowing
his little peculiarities I delighted in it and laughed
almost every time I saw it.

The decoration which stands near it is in its
own way equally interesting and characteristic.
It is a letter boldly framed, and which has an
easel also. It is not a very long letter nor a very
big one, but the handwriting is not in the least

cramped.   It has been allowed plenty of space and fills superbly a page and a half.   If one were inclined to criticise, one might say that it was large and sprawling, and that the lines had a tendency to emulate the example of the illustrious writer and go where they pleased.   But who would have the audacity and bad taste to criticise the very first literary effort of Illustrissimo Signor Bébé?   At the same time it seems a pity that it should be copied in mere common every-day printing instead of in the fearless and voluminous calligraphy of the author.

"CARA LUISA," it reads,

"Ti voglio bene e scrive meglio che posso—Torna presto e ti mando un bacio affezionatissimo.

"LUIGI ROBERTO."

In English it would be :—

"DEAR LOUISE,

"I wish thee very well"—(an Italian phrase which really signifies "I love you" in the sense that friends and parents and children say it to each other)—"and I write as well as I possibly can. Come back soon, and I send thee a very affectionate kiss.

"LOUIS ROBERT."

It was the very first letter of his life, written after the wonderful events of his first months at school where, after infinite diplomacy, he had finally been induced to permit himself to be escorted, with the full understanding that it was the beginning of his preparation for entering the Italian army, of which he had early announced his intention of becoming a general.

It had been composed by himself with many intellectual throes, and had been forwarded promptly to the young lady who had been the friend of his uneducated infancy, and who had delightedly told me the stories which had made him so distinct and amusing a little personage to me.

As he was only four years old when I first knew of him, and he was already quite a veteran, it may be argued that he had chosen his career of arms comparatively early in life.

I never knew exactly when he became a warrior or when he began to demand uniforms and carry swords and guns, and object eloquently and with fire to the wearing of long curls and petticoats, as unbecoming an officer and a gentleman, but nearly all the anecdotes I heard of him had for their point some such protest or demand as these.

His surroundings were not ordinary ones. He was born to the infant purple as it were. Emperors are supposed to issue mandates, czars are considered autocratic, kings and princes are regarded as having power, but for an omnipotent, uncombatable potentate, commend me to a beautiful, relative-worshipped baby who understands his privileges, and is not averse to using them.

Illustrissimo Signor Bébé was not in the least averse, and had fully appreciated his position from the first.

In the first place he was a marvellous beauty, in the second he had a will of iron braced with steel, in the third he had a beautiful and brilliant mother who adored him, and a father who adored her, and in the fourth he had taken prompt and decided possession of his entire family and their resources from his first hour.

He had two brothers who were unusually fine and clever, but Signor Bébé considered them merely as adjuncts which at times might be made useful. They were comparatively grown-up, and they had merely the accomplishments which could gain them admiration and prizes at school. They had short hair and wore ordinary clothes, and when they spoke only commanded ordinary attention. They were not attired in billows of lace under mantels of crimson plush; passers-by did not exclaim at the mere sight of their beauty; the moment they deigned to express an opinion or make a little dramatic gesture they did not find themselves attended by an enraptured and ecstatic audience.

" Il est à croquer, cet enfant," people exclaimed. " Joli comme un petit Amour avec ses longues boucles blondes et ses grands yeux noirs." (He is pretty enough to eat, that child, or to crunch between one's teeth like a bon-bon (to translate more exactly). He is as pretty as a little Love, with his long blonde curls and his big black eyes.)

Signor Bébé heard a great deal of French spoken, and spoke a little himself, but it must be confessed a very little. But this fact did not prejudice him when he desired to be sufficiently sweeping in his remarks to his poor, long-suffering, much-trampled-on German nurse.

" I speak only Italian, French and English," he said. " No German. I hate German. It is ugly and stupid. The Germans," with a scathing glance at poor Margarethe, " are all stupid and ugly too." Margarethe knew nothing but German, and did not in the least understand Italian. It was said to be rather a touching spectacle to see her calmly beaming and delighted countenance when the Illustrissimo " chivied " her in his mellifluous Tuscan, calling her, " Bruta, Imbecile, Stupida, Tedescacia," while she broadly smiled, imagining confidingly, it was said, that he was lavishing endearments upon her. She was a good, stupid soul, and was always ready to be his slave. It was she who dressed him laboriously, inserting one kicking, dancing foot into his sock, and then heavily and seriously giving chase all over the house, while he ran from one room to another, until she caught him and bore him back to his bedroom to put on the other. She ran miles during the performance of his toilet, and in warm weather ended it mopping her brows and exhausted, but still mildly beaming. It was she who was called upon to be the horse, and be enthusiastically and realistically beaten by the Illustrissimo, when he placed the chairs in a row to make a coach, and played coachman himself. It was she who must be drilled, and marched with an umbrella or poker over her shoulder, while the illustrious General Bébé rated her vigorously for the lack of promptness and soldierly grace in manœuvres.

It never occurred to the Illustrissimo that the whole world and the fulness thereof were not created solely that he might dispose of them for his own amusement. I do not think he ever asked for anything. Everything was given to him before he had time to ask. Apparently people sat up at night to invent things to give him. Superb playthings were lavished on him on every side. Wonderful uniforms, swords and guns and lances were made for him and sent by doting godparents and insatiate adorers in various cities. He was an officer of infantry, of cavalry, of engineers; he was a bersagliere with broad, low hat and floating plumes; he was a *cuirassier*, an *uhlan*, and, I believe, even a Papal Guard; everything military and bloodthirsty, and brilliant in accoutrements was Illustrissimo Signor Bébé. When a military idea occurred to him he simply ordered his nearest relatives to assist him to carry it out.

" To-day I saw an officer's funeral," he would perhaps announce in the middle of dinner. " There were soldiers marching and there were drums. They went like this, ' Buom, buom, buom,' " thumping solemnly on the table with the largest spoon he could appropriate. " There were flags and guns. The soldiers marched like this," scrambling down from his chair to illustrate with funereal dramatic action. " Papa—Godfredo—Oscarino—come and march. And we will have an officer's funeral. Papa, carry the fire-screen for a funeral banner, Godfredo carry the poker, and Oscarino the tongs. I will be the music—buom, buom, buom, that's the drum—tra lira la, that's the other musics."

And it was absolutely necessary that he should be followed solemnly round the table in funeral pomp, while the soup got cold.

" At least, show respect," he would say furiously to the brother who dared to giggle ; " it is a generale." I do not know what would have happened if his family had refused to form the procession, and had firmly continued eating their soup. I used to feel curious to know. But I never heard of such iconoclastic steps being taken.

But notwithstanding the processions, the uniforms and weapons, he felt there were serious obstacles in the way of his military career.

" Soldiers," he said, " do not wear long curls and petticoats. I have *never* seen one. What would they do on the field of battle ! *You*," sternly to his mamma, " have never seen a general in a frock and sash and with curls."

" Well—no," his mamma was obliged to admit reluctantly.

" The generale who rides by with the soldiers in the morning has no curls," he elaborated, "and he does not wear petticoats, I have noticed."

" But perhaps he did when he was your age," said his mother.

" I do not believe it. I shall salute him and ask him the next time I see him on the Lung Arno." And he walked up and down the salon gesticulating dramatically.

" Belli soldati, che portano le sottane e i riccioli." (Pretty soldiers, who wear petticoats and curls.) " Ma sì, signore, quando vedrò il generale—glielo voglio proprio domandare." (Yes, sirs, when I see the general I will indeed ask him.)

I should have been very much charmed to have had the privilege of being present during the interview, when the " generale " was put to the question. But I was not present on that interesting occasion, and I have only had the pleasure of imagining it.

I can see the Lungarno Nuova, almost dazzling white in the brilliant Italian sun and under the pure brightness of the blue sky. I can see the familiar, gaily costumed figures of the peasant women who stand always in the same place with their pile of queer, home-made stuffs and embroideries in purple and red and yellow and green. I can see the few morning promenaders, mostly *foresticri*, and children and nurses taking their slow walk by the low wall which borders the bank of the shallow, unreliable river Arno. I can see the old man with the old basket piled with violets and jonquils and daffodils and hyacinths, or deep blue and red anemones and delicate, shivering sprays and branches of yellow mimosa. I can hear his voice as he chants " Belli violi ! Belli violi ! Mammoli, belli mammoli." And as I listen I see Signor Bébé marching valiantly with a sword in his sash and poor Margarethe trying to keep up with him, because it is never the Illustrissimo who tries to keep up with *her*.

And in the distance there approaches a tall old officer with a martial tread and sword and spurs, and a fine grey moustache, and the uniform of a " Generale dei Carabinieri."

And the Illustrissimo catches sight of him and shrieks aloud with rapture.

" The generale," he says ; " come quick—come —run fast after me. I am going to ask him."

He flies, and his *boucles blondes* stream after him like a yellow silk banner; his shining sword dances, and the generale sees him and smiles, as people always do when they see Signor Bébé.

And I imagine how the generale looked and how his smile grew as the little figure drew up before him and bestowed upon him a most military salute.

"Generale," says the Illustrissimo boldly, "I told my mamma I would ask you. Do you ever wear petticoats and long curls?"

"Petticoats! curls! my dear!" exclaimed the old officer.

"I knew you did not; I have told my mamma. How can a soldier wear curls and petticoats? How could he fight and use his sword? I am a soldier! I am going to be a generale like you. And a pretty generale I should be with curls and frocks! My mamma must take them off. You do not wear them, do you?"

"No," said the generale, bending over him smiling; "I do not."

"Then I must not. No generale does. You *never* wore them, did you?"

"Well," admits the generale, smiling more than ever, "I think *perhaps* I did, when I was as young as you!"

"I am six!" cried the Illustrissimo grandly.

"*Six!*"

THE LITTLE FIGURE DREW UP BEFORE HIM AND BESTOWED UPON HIM
A MOST MILITARY SALUTE

" When you are sixteen," said the generale, patting the small hand he had taken, and nodding his head consolingly, " your curls will be cut off and you will not wear *sottane*."

I can imagine the consternation of poor Margarethe when she reached the field of action, and her tremulous " Scusi, scusi, Signor Generale," as she dragged her gesticulating, expostulating charge away.

It was after we had left Florence that the great decision was made that the Illustrissimo Signor must go to school. It must have been a decision arrived at with no small misgivings and with no trivial discussion in family conclave. It was not an insignificant matter, and there was always one most serious point to be considered. His papa and mamma, his grandmothers and godmothers might decide that he should go. But what if his decision did not accord with theirs ? What if Illustrissimo Bébé decided that he would not ? I can imagine how carefully the subject was broached, how diplomatically it was dealt with, and what a specious military air all scholastic training was given. I should have wished to have been present on these occasions also, but this too was a joyful experience denied me. I only heard that somehow military training skilfully interwoven with the alphabet and " pot hooks and hangers," and never being allowed to disconnect themselves in the Illustrissimo's mind, finally prevailed. There was a delightful legend that he required his mamma to go to school with him, and that this very charming and vivacious young person dutifully accompanied him daily to the seat of learning, and learned the alphabet also; but this seems really too delicious to be true, so I have always preferred to believe it, without inquiring into it too closely.

At any rate I know that at this time the despised *sottane* were finally cast aside with other unmilitary trivialities, the *boucles blondes* were cropped off, and, armed to the teeth, Illustrissimo Signor Bébé went to school. He never went without a sword, sometimes he took also a gun, and as many stilettos as could be stuck round his belt. It appeared that he regarded the field of letters as a field of battle, only to be entered in full panoply.

"Where is my sword?" he used to say at nine o'clock, as other children say, " Where is my spelling-book?"

We used to be entertained from time to time with animated descriptions of his educational progress. This, it appeared, was magnificent.

"You will be charmed to hear," his mamma wrote to his Cara Luisa, " that Bébé brings home always *des diplomes de sagesse* (diplomas for good behavior).

"It is rather a mystery, but it is no less true that he gains them."

We were charmed and also rather surprised. For myself, reflecting upon past anecdotes, I was a little inclined to think that in the case of the Illustrissimo, the pen might *not* be mightier than the sword. I suggested to Cara Luisa, that perhaps the sword induced the pen to inscribe these noteworthy certificates.

"Bébé gets always his *diplomes de sagesse*," wrote another friend of his family. "We don't quite understand why, as he stays at home from school whenever he is inclined to, which is generally."

It was at this time that the wonderful autograph letter was written which stands framed on the little table. I was thinking then of returning to visit Florence, and Cara Luisa spoke of this in answering the letter, and said that she would take to the Illustrissimo a veritable sailor costume which she could buy in London, the costume of "un vero capitano inglese." From this moment until we reached Florence, every visitor who entered the house was greeted at the door with the ecstatic and excited proclamation that "La Luisa, la Luisa" was coming back and was bringing him the costume of a real "capitano inglese." "La Luisa" took it, collar and anchors and cords and whistle, gold-banded cap and cutlass and all.

Among all his other uniforms he had never pos-
sessed this one. When she went to call, she
asked the servant politely for Signor Roberto,
and she was sitting alone in the salon when he
entered.

He had grown and lost his plumpness, he wore
a little coat, and his curls were cropped close to
his head, and his hair was no longer golden. But
he was still as ever Illustrissimo Signor Bébé.
He approached her holding out his hand to shake
hands in the proper English style, in deference
to her foreign sojourns.

" High do you do?" he remarked triumphantly. "High do you do, La Luisa? Do you spik
English, I spik English." And having exhausted
his vocabulary, he poured forth a volley of his
native Italian, the point of which was, of course,
his desire to put on immediately the costume of
the real English captain. His mamma thought
she had taught him to say, " How do you do,"
but the fact that it became " High do you do"
when he reached the salon was of small moment.
He felt himself perfectly at ease in his character
of linguist.

" And how about the *diplomes de sagesse*, Bébé?"
asked his visitor. " How do you get them, when
they tell me that you stay at home so often, and
scarcely go to school at all?"

He made a fine sweeping gesture of triumph.

"Yes," he said. "You see! there are some of those others who go every day and do not get any. And I—I who stay at home so many days, can still get one every time."

This, it was suggested later by a subtle mind, was perhaps an excellent reason, the sole occasions when the recipient was "sage" being when he was absent from the scene of his scholastic triumphs. When we were in Rome a few weeks later "La Luisa" received a photograph. It represented a small English naval officer with a small Italian face, apparently seated on the shore of the boundless ocean, and looking most nautically into the "offing" whatsoever the "offing" may be.

Its place is on the table near the framed letter, and under it is written :—

"Illustrissimo Signor Bébé, qui regarde son navire."

7

THE DAUGHTER OF THE CUSTODIAN

THE DAUGHTER OF THE CUSTODIAN

THE guide book only mentions her father, but we did not see her father, we only saw her, and I was glad it was so. I dare say her father is a very nice old Roman peasant, but she performed his duties in a much more interesting way than he could have done, I am sure, and she was such a pretty, sweet-voiced, friendly, smiling little thing that it was a pleasure to walk round the old Roman cemetery guided by her, and listening to her soft Italian chatter.

It was chatter, and bright childish chatter too, and one certainly never saw a brighter pair of dark eyes or a happier little face, and yet she lives under the shadow of the dark cypresses in an old deserted graveyard; when she sees the sunshine in the morning she sees it first piercing through these shadowy cypress trees to dapple kindly the old grey moss-grown monuments and granite slabs, and I suppose she has played among the mounds of earth since her very babyhood.

It is in the old Protestant cemetery outside

Rome that she lives, in the small house just near the big iron gates which are always kept locked until some visitor rings the queerly tinkling little bell which hangs outside, and either the child or her father the custodian goes to open it, and shows the strangers the graves they have come to see.

It is quite an old cemetery. It was laid out at the beginning of the century, but is no longer used to bury people in, but strangers who are in Rome —particularly English and Americans—nearly all go there just to stand and look at two graves.

They are the graves of two great English poets, both of whom had sad lives, both of whom died sad deaths, and both of whom all the world knows and all the world remembers.

They are the poets Shelley and Keats. It was these graves I went to see and which the custodian's little daughter guided me to with my English lady friend and my Italian companion.

It was a lovely day in the very early spring when we drove out to the cemetery, but in spite of the sunshine it looked rather dark under all the tall cypresses as our carriage stopped before the gate.

"The gate seems to be locked," I said. "Perhaps we have not come at the right hour."

"I suppose one must ring the bell," said my companion. "Evidently one must. You see the chain hangs outside."

So she got out of the carriage and pulled the chain; the bell gave its queer cracked tinkle and almost immediately the little girl came out of the house and ran towards us with a big key.

She opened the gates and stood smiling up at us as we entered, as if we had been guests she had been expecting and was very pleased to see. It was evident that her father was away, and that she had been left to perform his duties.

"Buon giorno, Signore," she said sweetly, and we all three smiled back at her and said "Buon giorno" in return.

She was not more than eight or nine years old at the most, and at first I thought that as she was so young she perhaps might not know the name of Shelley, or might not remember it as it was English and she was only used to hearing Italian words.

"Ask her," I said to my companion, "to show us the grave where the great English poet is buried. So many people come to see it that of course she will have heard it spoken of often enough to have remembered. She will not know the name perhaps, if you mention it, but she will know there is the grave of an English poet, which the *forestieri* always want to see."

But I need not have had any doubts. The moment my companion spoke of the "Poeta inglese" her pretty little face lighted up and her bright dark eyes smiled more brightly than ever.

"Sì, sì, Signora!" she exclaimed. "Shelli—Shelli!"

She made it an Italian name—giving it an Italian termination, but it was clear that she knew all about it.

She led the way, running lightly before us up a rather steep path between the graves until she turned a corner and presently stopped triumphantly before a deserted-looking nook near a dark grey moss and lichen covered wall.

"Shelli," she said, waving her little hand and smiling brilliantly, "Shelli."

And before us, among the graves and under the cypresses, there was a slab of dark granite fitted into the earth, and all that I remember now of the inscription (which I think was in Latin) is the name Percy Bysshe Shelley. Those of the children who know of this poet will remember how he was overtaken by a squall while in a boat with his friend at sea, and how his body was afterwards washed ashore in the Bay of Spezia, and burned there on a funeral pyre on the sands, his friend Lord Byron looking on as mourner. But his heart would not burn, and it is his heart only which lies under the stone slab in that shady corner outside Rome—his strange, wild, ardent, often troubled poet's heart. It prompted him to do many things which were against the world's laws and which the world blames, but I have always thought that in the depths of this heart which would not burn when his body fell to ashes, he truly believed—whether he was mistaken or not —that he was right, and that mightier laws not of this world would understand him and blame him less.

We stood in the cypress-shadowed corner for a while, looking at the grave and talking to each other about it, our small guide regarding us with great interest, and now and then volunteering some friendly explanation in Italian.

A great many *foresticri* came to see this grave, she told us. Oh, a great many! And it was only a heart that was buried there. Her father had told her. It was the heart of a great English milord who had written books which everybody read. He had been drowned, and his body had been burned at Spezia, by the sea which drowned him, but his heart had not been burnt, and was brought here.

"Ask her if there is any other grave here that the *foresticri* wish to see," I said to my companion.

She looked as animated as she had done when we asked her about Shelley. She looked as if she were quite delighted at having something else to show us which we should be sure to be interested in.

"Keatsi," she said in her droll little Italian way. "Keatsi."

"She means Keats," I exclaimed. "I did not know that his grave was in this particular cemetery."

It was not in this particular cemetery it seemed. This was the "Old Cemetery," but there was the other cemetery only a few yards away, and the grave of "Keatsi," as she called him, was there.

We said good-by to the slab of granite and followed her down the steep path again and through the iron gateway, across the road and over some grass until we came to a curious narrow entrance which led us into the "altro cimitero." Quite near the entrance were two graves with white headstones, side by side, and very close together.

"Keatsi," said the custodian's little daughter, pointing to the nearest, and her pretty exultant smile showed that she at least did not know anything of the sad story of the broken poet's heart that had long ago changed to dust beneath.

There was no name written on this headstone; only these sorrowful words:—

" This grave contains all that was mortal of a young English poet, who, on his death-bed, in the bitterness of his heart, desired these words to be engraved on his tombstone—

' Here lies one whose name was writ in water.'"

His was such a cruel story. He was so young, so sensitive, so full of dreams and ambitions. He himself must have known *surely* that immortal genius burned in his heart and brain, and that from glowing genius all his dreaming sprang. He poured forth his whole life and strength into his work, and then, as the sole return, suffered the mortal anguish of seeing it scorned, derided, and condemned by the inhospitable, uncomprehending world. Then a fatal disease—consumption, that most cruel and hopeless disease of all — slowly drained his life and courage to the dregs. At first he struggled against it—perhaps he could not believe that this last blow had really come, it must have seemed too hard—but when he died in Rome, alone save for his one true generous friend, his spirit was broken, his poet wings hung shattered, he could hope and dream no more.

"Let it be graven on my tombstone," he said in weary bitterness, "'Here lies one whose name was writ in water.'"

It seemed to him that his life, his labor, his genius, had all gone for nothing—they would not even leave a ripple on the great sweeping river of Time. And yet he had so suffered and so fiercely aspired. If he had only known what Fame would give to him too late, that pilgrim feet would stand by his grave without a name, that the name not written on the plain headstone would blaze in letters of golden fire on the page where only the names of the Immortals burn.

And by his side—close by his side—lies that one generous, faithful friend who was true to him and tried to comfort him through all his anguish and loneliness, when he was poor, despised, and desolate, when he went down into the Valley of the Shadow of Death, in a foreign land, helpless and otherwise as it seemed utterly alone.

It seemed so fitting that he should lie there, so beautiful. It is such a great and noble thing to be a faithful friend. Surely there can be nothing greater and sweeter than to be this one lovable thing. To be faithful and a comfort through failure, grief, misfortune, discouragement, illness, even to the gates of death. All this Joseph Severn was to John Keats, and because of this his name, too, is written in gold upon the page of the immortal ones. One cannot remember the one without the other, one cannot lay flowers upon the grave of one without scattering them upon the turf growing above the kind, true heart of the other. The kind, faithful heart is as great as the marvellous genius which so burned and glowed that it can never be forgotten.

And on this second headstone are written words which touch one's heart as deeply as those on the grave without a name, but they move one in a happier way.

"To the memory of Joseph Severn, devoted

friend and death-bed companion of John Keats, whom he lived to see numbered among the immortal poets of England."

It seemed like a happy ending to a sad story. Through the long anxious days of growing illness and pain, made heavier by blighted hopes and ambitions, Joseph Severn kept near his friend. It was he who was with him when he saw the blood upon the handkerchief he had held to his lips, and said, " I know the color of that blood. It is arterial blood. It is my death warrant." It was he who, watching him through the dreadful exhausted nights, when his hair was dank with cold, heavy sweat, sketched, while he lay in one of his deep, death-like sleeps, the face lying upon the pillow which is reproduced as the frontispiece of his poems. It was he who heard his earliest plaints, and watched him until the very end, when he died, believing that his poor life had been a broken bubble gone for nought. But Severn lived many years afterwards. He saw the ripening of the harvest his poor friend never gathered, and he rejoiced while he mourned for him, and felt his own life more complete, and worth the living. It must have seemed to him that it was almost *his* harvest too.

An artist—" eminent for his representation of Italian life and nature," his headstone tells us— " British Consul of Rome, and officer of the

Crown of Italy in recognition of his services to
Freedom and Humanity."

He lived a fine and useful life of his own, he
had an art and a career; he lived to be an old
man, but I think that perhaps in the depths of his
generous heart he liked best to think of himself
as the faithful friend whom poor John Keats
clung to, and looked last on when he died.

His headstone was erected by a number of people, who loved and revered the memory of the
friend who was so gentle and so true.

And it touched and pleased me so much to see
that the list engraved upon the back of the stone
was headed with names all Americans know and
are proud of.

As I passed round to read these I laid my hand
softly on the stone without a name when my companions were not looking.

"You are immortal now," I said. And afterwards I touched even more softly the headstone
placed so near.

"Constant friend," I thought, "true heart; who
does not love you and is not grateful? You will
not be forgotten either."

. . . . . .

The custodian's little daughter did not know
the story the turf covered. I dare say she often
wondered why the *foresticri* were so fond of visiting the graves of signori who wrote books, why

they laid so many violets on them, and sometimes carried away a leaf, or a few blades of grass as if they were precious, and why, above all, they looked sad and reverent, and spoke to each other in such low tones, as if the poet, who had been buried a lifetime ago, was some near friend who had just been covered with the earth.

But she had seen it all so often that she was quite accustomed to it, and usually occupied her time in innocent inspection and admiration of the pretty things the signoras wore. She had spent her little life under the cypresses and among the graves, and they seemed to her quite ordinary surroundings. While I was standing by the first grave I felt something touch me gently, even caressingly. The child had drawn quite near me, and it was her small hand. Bright as the day was, it was rather cold while driving, and I wore a long black plush mantle, which was bordered with soft black fox fur, and which had very long sleeves of a heavy brocade that fell from my shoulders to the bottom of the cloak. It was this which had attracted her attention, and she had put her little hand out, and was stroking the plush and fur.

"Molto, molto bella" (very, very beautiful), I heard her whisper quite reverently to herself.

The little hand felt so gentle and caressing, and she seemed so pleased, that I leaned a little nearer to her and then looked down into her pretty childish face and smiled, so that she would know I did not mind her caressing what she thought so nice. She understood what the little movement and smile meant, and she looked simply delighted. She gave herself up to examining me, touching the plush and fur admiringly, and lifting the long, falling sleeves to look at the heavy brocade, talking softly to herself in Italian all the time.

"But what a beautiful mantle," she whispered. "I have never seen such a beautiful thing. This that it is made of is far more splendid than velvet; it is so soft and thick. And what long, soft fur; and so much. The Signora must be a very grand lady. And what beautiful, soft feathers all round her hat!"

I did not hear her say all this myself. I only heard the "Molto, molto bella," and noticed that she continued whispering as she stroked my cloak. It was my Italian companion who heard her, and told me afterwards.

She turned to this lady next, I heard, and found a great deal to admire in her attire. She wore a black cloth dress, which was trimmed with black and gold, and it was this trimming our small guide found so splendid.

"You—you are dressed in gold," she said: "in real gold. And you have even a bonnet like your dress. The blonde Signora is dressed all in soft fur and something that is much more beautiful than velvet; and you are in gold. How rich you must be!"

Then, my companion told me, she looked from one to the other of us curiously, and rather pityingly.

"But you have no earrings," she said. "Why have you no earrings?"

"We do not wear them," answered the young lady.

"I have earrings," the child said; "I wear them always." And she touched the large gold hoops in her ears. "How strange that the Signore who are so rich and have such beautiful clothes do not wear any!"

I do not know whether she thought that we might be a little mad—as the *foresticri* sometimes were—or whether the idea suggested itself to her that we had spent all our money on real gold frocks and stuffs that were more splendid than velvet, but it is certain that she felt sorry for us. Quite a gleam of light relieved her expression as she looked at my English friend and pointed to her ears.

"But the other Signora," she exclaimed, "she has earrings!"

One of us at least had earrings, and that somewhat lightened her innocent anxiety. Bright as her smiling, dark-eyed face was, and lightly as she

8

tripped before us to lead the way, she did not look very strong, and I could not help noticing that she had rather a troublesome cough.

"Have you any brothers and sisters?" we asked.

"Not now," she answered. "There were seven of us; but all have died but me. One baby died only a month ago."

"You have a bad cough," my companion had said, as we were crossing from one cemetery to the other.

"Una tossa nervosa" (a nervous cough), she said, quite cheerfully.

"But you must take care of it, and not let it get worse."

Before I returned to the carriage I put some pieces of silver in her little hand. One always gives money to a custodian, and it pleased me to put more in the small hand than I should have placed in the larger one.

"Grazie tante, Signora! Grazie tante!" she said, looking up at me with the prettiest possible of brilliant smiles. "Buon giorno."

She ran away in the sunshine, turning to smile again and nod her little dark head to us gaily and gratefully. Her mother was waiting for her, and we saw the child showing her the money with delighted gestures. They were standing away from the cypresses, outside of the grey walls, in the bright, warm Italian sunshine. And I was glad as I drove away that it was in the brightness and not in the shadow that I saw the last of the childish figure of the custodian's little daughter.

A PRETTY ROMAN BEGGAR

A PRETTY ROMAN BEGGAR

THE dearest thing I saw in Florence the last time I was there, was a delightful little American boy of seven, and one of the most charming and suggestive in Rome was a small fellow about the same age, who sat surrounded by the stately wonders and spaces of St. Peter's, his bright, eager, thoughtful child face upturned to his mother and father, who were sitting and talking together near him. I have become quite clever in recognizing American and English faces, and I knew this little boy was an American, and there was something in his clear, wide-awake eyes that made me want to stop before him and hold out my hand and say :

" Come with me, and I will show you the wonderful old places I know so well, and we will tell each other stories about them. We can make marvellous stories in almost every street, and I shall find out all sorts of new things when I see the temples and palaces and great ruins through your seven-year-old American eyes."

But, as we were quite strangers to each other,

I could only smile at him and pass him by. I had been sent away from London by my doctors, because I had been ill for a long time after an accident I had met with in the autumn when I had been thrown out of my carriage and dangerously hurt. They said that London fogs were bad for me, and I must travel where I could see the blue sky and the sun. So I went to the south of France and to Italy, and that is why I went to Rome, which is one of the cities I love best of all.

I wanted to be quiet, so I went to a hotel which an English Roman told me afterwards was "the oldest, the most respectable, and the dullest in Rome." But that exactly pleased me, and I could not be dull with three interesting people with me and all old Rome around me. I liked the old hotel. I liked my apartments and my comfortable salon, with the mysterious frescos on the ceiling—the frescos we were always trying to explain to each other, as if they were conundrums. Especially I was fond of the old square with the elephant bearing an obelisk on its back in the centre, and the hoary, wonderful old Pantheon at the corner.

It was in this square I learned to know my pretty beggar whom I want to make a tiny sketch of to hang in my gallery of children. My little Roman, so far as beauty goes, is one of the most perfect small pictures I remember, and he is

chiefly interesting as a study because he belongs
to a profession which I think does not really exist
in America, and because I was so curious to
know what thoughts there were behind his beautiful child eyes, or if it could be that there were
no definite thoughts at all.

He was a professional beggar and a professional
beauty, and, though he was only five years old, it
was quite plain that he knew perfectly well what
an assistance to the first profession the last one
was. He would have been taught to beg if he
had not been handsome at all, but I am sure he
knew that he would not have had so many patrons, or half so many *soldi* if he had not been so
pretty to look at. To a stranger it seems that
every Roman child who is not rich is taught to
regard begging as a sort of honest industry which
any useful infant will cultivate. After one becomes somewhat accustomed to the swarms of
little boys and girls who rush to one's carriage
when it stops before a church or palace and
scramble clamoring up the long flights of steps
after one, they begin to be even a little amusing.
They do not look the least uncomfortable or
hungry, some of them are pretty, and often they
are picturesque because they are dressed in
the Roman peasants' dress, in the hope that some
artist will want to put them in a picture and pay
them for sitting as models. And they generally

appear to be amusing themselves together, and seem to find it rather a joke to chase after these princely strangers who have nothing better to do than drive about and look at churches and pictures and ruins. I am convinced that they think us great simpletons, but they would be sorry to see us wiser because that would make their profession less lucrative. It is their cheerful audacity which makes one smile at last. They know the *forestieri* so well (*forestieri* is the Italian word for "foreigners"). They know that a rather shy or inexperienced one will feel that if a bouquet of violets is forced into his or her hand it must be paid for, so violets are thrown into one's carriages, little clusters are forcibly attached to the coats of masculine passers-by, and it is only when one has become quite hardened that one discovers how to toss them back into the small basket with an amiable smile and " Non, grazie, non." There is another thing they have learned, which is that even the *forestieri* who do not understand Italian are more than likely to know French, so some of the smallest ones have been taught one or perhaps two mournful French phrases which they say over and over again as they run after one. I shall not soon forget a plump, well-fed, cheerful little girl in a gay apron and Roman head-gear, who trotted after me up and down a long flight of steps near the Pincio, saying as fast as she could

"Je meurs de faim, je meurs de faim," which is the French for "I die of hunger, I die of hunger."

"You little story-teller," said the English lady who was with me. "You are stuffed as full of macaroni as you can possibly be." And, though she spoke English, the child evidently recognized that she had not produced her effect on these "Inglesi," for she gave us up as a bad investment, with a sly little smile.

I suppose my pretty beggar boy had been a model as well as a beggar ever since he could walk, perhaps even before. His mother and the woman who was always with her were evidently models when they had good fortune. They were handsome women who wore the picturesque Roman dress, and sat or stood in the sun in the old square, with baskets of violets near them, which they professed to sell. About them played my pretty little Roman and his companion, who was about the same age as himself, and almost equally pretty. Both of them were dressed like small copies of picturesque bandits on the stage; they had short, bright-colored jackets and knee-breeches, and bands crossed round their legs, and both had broad-brimmed, rather pointed hats of soft felt on their full, silky, curling hair.

They were both charming, but my little fellow was either the bolder or the prettier or the more coaxing of the two, I don't know which it was;

but somehow he always seemed to know quite
well that he was my favorite. He had such soft,
round cheeks, the color of a very ripe peach—an
Indian peach, perhaps, with the red showing
through the downy brown; he had such a dim-
pling laugh, and such large, soft brown eyes, and
such a lot of thick, chestnut brown curls. His
curls looked soft, too; he looked soft and warm
all over, as if he would feel like a rabbit or a
squirrel, if one took him in one's arms.

The first time I saw him was one afternoon
when I was going to drive to the Pincio to hear
the band which plays there every day from four
to six.

My carriage used to wait in the courtyard until
I came down the stairs and got into it at the foot
of them; but this day, after we had driven
through the entrance into the square, we had to
send for a cushion or something which had been
forgotten, and so we waited and my pretty
beggar saw us.

He was very faithful to the exigencies of his
profession. I noticed afterward that he always
stopped playing when he saw any one approaching to whom his business instincts taught him he
might apply, and he always trotted after them
quite far enough to give them a fair trial. So,
seeing the carriage with the two horses and a
comparatively resplendent coachman waiting

before the courtyard entrance of the big hotel, and seeing that it contained *forestieri*—ladies in velvet and furs, one of whom leaned against a crimson silk cushion, he felt that this was a business opportunity not to be neglected, and came running across the square followed by his companions. I suppose it was the crimson cushion which caused him to single me out, or perhaps he had seen me smiling at his prettiness as he ran towards us in the sun—certainly both he and his friend directed their active attention to me.

Only a little Italian beggar, and a professional beauty at that, could have begged as he did — with such gayety and coaxing, and such perfect freedom and friendliness. It was not his *rôle* to say "Je meurs de faim "—his was a comedy part and in the company of two he was the " leading gentleman," because, though his companion was *almost* as pretty as he, and did the same things and repeated the same words, one felt sure he had not originated them; I had an idea that he admired his friend very much, and respected his professional talents immensely, and adored him.

"Bella signora," they both clamored gayly showing their white teeth and dimples, and jumping up and down, holding out little soft brown palms. " Bella signora, uno soldino—uno soldino; via, bella signora, uno soldino " (Beautiful lady, a

little penny—a little penny ; oh, come now, beautiful lady, a little penny).

" Via " does not literally mean " Oh, come now,"
but I think that is the only way to put it into
English when a little beggar says it in that coaxing, expostulatory way.   Nothing could possibly
have been more coaxing than that " via."   He
made it express so much.   " Oh, come now," it
seemed to say, " you are a miladi inglese.   You
go out in a grand carriage with the big horses.
You drive to the Pincio and listen to the music.
You have a purse full of little pennies and silver
pieces in your pocket.   And see how pretty I
am, and soft and bright my eyes are when I
laugh at you.   Oh, come now, what do little pennies matter to miladies like you ?"

And he laughed all the time, and looked at me
with such gay confidence in my friendliness and
admiration.   I suppose he had studied faces too
long not to understand the sort of smile that
meant at least two or three *soldi*.   I am always
being told it is wrong to encourage beggars, but
I am afraid I do encourage them disgracefully
sometimes.   I took a nice handful of *soldi* out of
my purse and bent over the side of the carriage ;
half I put into one soft little brown paw and half
into the other, laughing into the bright mellow
dark eyes that laughed back at me, and when I
put the coins down I gave each dusky soft paw a

"BELLA SIGNORA, UNO SOLDINO!"

little pat. I could not remember that these were small professional beggars. It seemed as if Boy and the Socialist were five years old again, and their lovely mops of hair were dark instead of golden, and they were dancing about begging for pennies. No little beggars could have been bolder or gayer, or more assured than Boy or Socialist were. They were quite professional as far as I was concerned, and they were always sure they would get their *soldini*. What an astonishing thing it would have seemed to the passers-by to have seen a Signora Inglese take a little Roman beggar suddenly in her arms, hold him on her knee and kiss his velvet cheeks—but to me that would have seemed the most natural thing to do. These two did not often have so many *soldi* given them at once, it was evident. They looked so delightful and laughed so, and gave such triumphant little hops as they clamored, " Grazie, Signora, grazie, grazie!" ("Thank you, lady, thank you, thank you.") And then they took each other's hands and scampered across the square together. Of course I looked after them. I could not help it. And when they reached the corner near the Pantheon the " leading gentleman " had one of his pretty inspirations. He checked his run for a moment, and wheeled round, still holding his companion's hand, and with the most graceful little smiling gestures he threw me a whole butterfly flight of kisses and his friend did the same.

"Ah, how pretty!" said someone in the carriage. "Only a little Italian beggar could do that. Imagine a London crossing sweeper throwing one kisses when one gave him a ' brown.' "

If I had been able to remain in Rome, as I had planned to do, I should have had the opportunity of knowing more of my fascinating little beggar. *Soldi* and smiles every day for a few weeks would certainly have made us quite intimate, and I could have talked to him quite freely. I had intended to remain in Rome until after the Easter fêtes and ceremonies, and I was beginning to feel very well and happy in those first beautiful sunshine and flower-flooded days of the early Roman spring. But I received a letter one morning which set me in a few hours on my way to America, and two weeks from then my pretty Roman beggar was thousands of miles away, and I walked into a bedroom in my house in Washington where a boy with eyes as dark as his lay waiting for me with cheeks and hands hot with fever.

But before the letter came I had seen my little beggar every day. Every time my carriage passed out of the courtyard of the hotel he came running for his *soldini* in the most delightful spirits ; every day he and his companion laughed and danced and showed their dimples and white

teeth and kissed their hands, and every day I was
rather tempted to coax the "leading gentleman"
into my carriage and take him on my knee for a
drive on the Pincio.   I wanted also to take him to
a grand confectioner's on the Corso, and say to
him: "You may have whatever you like."   I
wonder if he would have quite lost his little wits
with wonder and delight, or if he would have been
practical enough to fill his bright-colored bandit's
jacket with sufficient indigestion to cast a slight
glow over the remainder of his existence after he
had recovered from it.

My companion always used to say a few words
to him for me, when I gave him his *soldini*.

"Do you know," she asked him one day, "why
it is that the *signora bionda* gives you so many
soldi ?"

He smiled charmingly, but shook his head,—
"No, signora."

"It is because she has two *bambini* of her own,
and just now they are far, far away in America,
and she cannot give them *soldi*, so she gives them
to you.   The *signora bionda* loves *bambini*."

I was quite sure that he looked at the statement
in a purely professional light, and was not the
least sentimental in his views of it.   It was evident
to him that this miladi inglese or americana had
an amiable weakness which might be cultivated
and made most useful.   The "*due bambini*" were

certainly to be relied upon as a source of indefinite *soldi* if the memory of them were encouraged with smiles and little dancing skips, and plenty of kisses thrown gracefully and with intention. He was so far exhilarated at the prospect that he beamed all over and threw me charming kisses at once. And the next time he did not wait for the carriage, but seeing me leave the hotel on foot, he ran after me with greater confidence than ever.

" Do you intend to beg always?" I asked, either that time or the next that he followed us. " When you are older, you will be strong enough to work, for yourself. You will be too strong to beg. Don't you think so?"

It was at that moment I wished I could have seen the workings of his mind. I wanted so much to know what he thought.

But it was not possible to tell. Perhaps he thought the signora inglese was making a little joke and he ought to smile at it as a compliment —or perhaps he did not wish to commit himself for fear of saying the wrong thing to such excellent patrons. At any rate he smiled and looked up at us both in his prettiest way and with his gayest air. A smile like his—as ready and bright and soft, and unprejudiced—was a fortune in itself. At least he was quite aware of that.

I do not know whether I have made a sketch of him which will make him seem real to those

who read it, but he is a very real thing to me
though I barely understood a few sentences of his
language. There was some soft brightness in his
mellow eyes I understood, and something in his
childish beautiful face which somehow spoke to
my heart, and I cannot help believing that he will
not always be a beggar, but will find something
for his dusky little hands to do when they are
bigger, and that the magnetism and cleverness
which made him always the leader will make a
place for him a man need not be ashamed to fill.

EIGHT LITTLE PRINCES

EIGHT LITTLE PRINCES

ONE sees them in all the photograph shops in all the principal cities in Europe. Sometimes they are babies in lace frocks, sometimes they are little boys in sailor suits, and sometimes, though they are little fellows, they are dressed in military uniforms and are drawing themselves up and making a fine salute to some one regal or to the regiments they are supposed to command. I am very fond of photograph shops, and when I see a picture of any of the little princes I cannot waste my time on kings and queens and emperors until I have looked well at my little man and made up my mind that he looks happy, and as if he enjoyed himself and did not mind being a prince at all. One knows by heart the faces of kings and queens and emperors and empresses, but the little princes change each year, and occasionally there is a tiny new one, and that is very interesting.

I made the intimate acquaintance of five delightful happy-looking plump ones in the shops in the street by the Alster - Bassin, in Hamburg.

There was one I even chose at once for my favorite. I saw them again and again in Berlin, and drove by their palace, and looked up at their nursery windows, with the bars before them to keep the very little ones from tumbling out ; and I have seen their pictures so often during these last few days at Prague that I have become quite fond of them, and yesterday I went into a shop and bought photographs of them in all sorts of poses, and they are lying on my desk as I write.

These five are the children of the present young Emperor of Germany ; their grandmother was the Princess Royal of England, and so their great-grandmother is Queen Victoria.

On the day of the great Jubilee procession and ceremonials in London, when Boy and the Social-ist and I sat and watched the kings and queens and princes and princesses pass by in the midst of the music and great pageant, there was one tall superb horseman in a splendid white and gold uni-form, who was cheered loudly and enthusiastically, and whom everyone admired. " What a hand-some fellow," everyone said. " He is the most royal-looking of all."   He was the Crown Prince of Germany, the son of the good old Emperor William, and strong and splendid as he looked he was even then stricken with the dreadful malady which ended in his death not many months later, though in those few months the old Emperor died, and this son when he died was the Emperor himself.

It is his son who is the father of the five little princes I am becoming fond of. I think he must be a nice young father and love his five boys. I am sure their young mamma is very fond of them, too. She has a loving, motherly face, and I am convinced that when she has her five boys round her—as she nearly always has in the photographs —she never remembers she is an Empress at all.

I do not know the names of these little princes —at least I only know the name of the one who is my favorite. He became my favorite when I saw a darling picture of him in Hamburg. He is a beautiful little fellow, with a round face and laughing eyes, and a great deal of curly soft blonde hair. In the photograph he was dressed in a pretty white sailor suit, with a blue collar and cuffs, and he had short socks on his sturdy little legs, and was gambolling along gayly before his mamma in a stately park or garden. Perhaps it was in the park at Potsdam.

I always looked for him in all the picture shops, and I always found him in some prominent place in his white sailor suit, all dimples and smiles and curly fair hair. His name, I find, is Eitel, and he is next in age to the little Crown Prince, who, though he is not much bigger, has no curls, and is graver and always wears a uniform.

I have before me five photographs of these small German princes, which please me immensely. They please me because they look so happy, and as if they were loved and cared for, not because they are the children of an Emperor and Empress, but because they are dear little fellows.

The one which perhaps amuses me the most is called Unsere Hohenzollern, which means Our Hohenzollerns, Hohenzollern being the name of the Emperor's family.

This photograph is that of a handsome room which the young Emperor is just entering. The Empress is sitting in an easy chair, and on her knee is lying a tiny baby, evidently the very youngest princeling of the five. He is so very new a baby that he is lying in his *porte-enfant*, which is a sort of dainty lace and ribbon-trimmed cushion on which very young babies in most Continental countries are bound. His mamma is bending over and looking at him as every mamma looks at her baby—as the mothers of all the children who read this sketch used to look at them—as I used to look at Boy and the Socialist before they had any hair worth mentioning, or dreamed of wanting dynamos and electric motors.

The Emperor has just passed through the *por-tières*, and he is—as always—in uniform, and he is smiling as if he were very much amused. I know what it is that amuses him. It is the two very little princes who are next in age to the baby, and who are standing on their mamma's left hand near her knee. Pretty Eitel, with his sailor suit and curls, is on her right, with his brother, the Crown Prince. They look very grand indeed. The little Crown Prince is in uniform, and wears a sword. His left hand rests on his sword's hilt, and both he and pretty Eitel are standing very straight with their heels together, and are greeting their papa with a military salute.

It appears that if your papa is an Emperor—which does not often happen in America—when you see him you must salute him. Of course I have no doubt you may kiss him afterwards, but he is your Emperor as well as your papa, and you must salute him first. (I cannot tell you how pretty Eitel's bare legs in his short socks look drawn together in that grand military way. They are quite warlike.)

But the next to the youngest baby is only in white frocks, and sashes and bows on his shoulders, and is so young that he possibly does not know what an Emperor means or why one should feel it polite to scramble up from one's Noah's Ark and draw one's fat legs straight and put one's hand to one's forehead when one's papa comes into the room. But his brother, who is the next to the next from the baby, and who is perhaps even as much as four years old, has more experience and a greater sense of propriety, and while he is making his own little salute he is lifting his baby brother's hand and showing him how to put it to his forehead.

"See," he seems to be saying, "when papa comes in you must put your hand up like this. You must salute him.   That is a salute."

And I am sure that is what the young Emperor Papa is laughing at as he looks down at these two, and in a minute—out of the photograph—he will kiss them both.

There is another picture where the Emperor looks very nice. It is Christmas Eve, and one sees a large table with a splendid Christmas tree. It is lighted and loaded with presents, and on the table are trains of cars and books, and all sorts of charming things.   I can read the title of one big book.   It is " Militair Bilderbuch."   It is full of pictures of military scenes, I suppose.   The Germans are a nation of soldiers.   One little prince sits on a spirited rocking-horse with a drawn sword over his shoulder.   He looks as if he were going to prance into battle immediately.   The Empress has one arm round the Crown Prince, one round her fourth baby, and pretty Eitel stands before her showing her a box full of soldiers.   Just near her stands the Emperor, and he is taking a toy trumpet from the Christmas tree and is going to give it to the baby he has on his arm, and who has grown out of his *porte-enfant* and has hair, and a sash, and holds out his hands joyfully for the trumpet.

In another picture, which is called " Das neue Bruderchen " (the new little brother) the Empress is showing the new baby Prince to the other four, who are all crowding round him. There are soldiers and cannons on the floor, and the spirited rocking-horse has stopped prancing, and is looking on gravely, even thoughtfully. In another all five are round a table. The Crown Prince stands, the baby sits with a cushion behind him and plays on a drum, while pretty Eitel fires a cannon at a fortress, most valiantly defended by lead soldiers, who would evidently rather perish than surrender. That picture is called " Unsere Lieblinge," which means " Our Darlings." There is still another where pretty Eitel and his brother sit in a boat on an ornamental lake, while their papa stands with their mamma looking on, and taking care of two younger ones. I have one, too, of the Emperor with his little soldier Crown Prince leaning against his knee— and there is yet another where they ride on horseback side by side. I have studied all these pictures, and I am quite sure that these five little princes are not only happy and loved in photographs, but when they are in their own homes and are simply little boys and not an Emperor's sons.

I have two pictures of another Prince, but he is older than the little Germans, and he has a dark, handsome face, with a rather sad and thoughtful look—particularly in the last picture where his boyish sailor suit and hat are laid aside, and he is in uniform, and leaning on his sword.

I have been interested in him because I know he has not been a happy little prince, and I am afraid he cannot be a happy young king. The winter of the jubilee year I took Boy and the Socialist to Italy. Boy had been there before, but the Socialist had not, and that time I took them for a special reason. I had heard of a wonderful French school which had been established forty years, and whose master, a fine old Frenchman, had prepared boys for colleges in England, in France, in Germany, and in America. It seemed a droll thing to go to Florence that one's boys might learn French, but I had heard such fine things of this old master's affectionate, strong generalship of his pupils, that I made this long journey and sent my boys to him.

It was then I began to see this young prince, and be interested in him.

He was the young prince of Servia, and the fine old Frenchman taught him also, so we naturally should have heard of him even if we had not seen him. But we saw him often. Poor boy, he had a bad father and a beautiful mother, who was made very unhappy. She was Queen Natalie, and she was young and lovely, and adored her boy, and had, indeed, we heard, come to Florence because she wished to take care of him herself, and not let him remain exposed to the example of unmanliness and evil. It was very sad. It seemed that between father and mother there was always a struggle for the poor little prince, but it was his beautiful mother he loved and wished to be with.

He was always with her. We had our "Appartamento Mobiliato" in a large house on the Lungarno Nuovo, and in its big courtyard was the Russian church. The poor Queen Natalie was very devout, and went very often to church, and the young prince always went with her. He was about twelve years old, a tall, slender boy, with soft dark eyes like his mother's. We used to hear the carriage roll into the courtyard, and then we often looked out of the dining-room window and saw the two get out and go into the church together. Quite near us was the Cascine, the beautiful park by the river Arno, which is the fashionable drive and promenade, and where on Sunday the military band plays. When we drove there we often saw the prince and his mother, and more than once we passed them as they walked side by side.

When Queen Natalie returned to Servia, which
is a small royalty that is dependent upon Russia,
the struggle between herself and King Milan—
the prince's father — began more fiercely than
ever. The Queen Natalie was exiled from Servia, and Prince Alexander taken from her. But
he was not happy away from his mother ; he was
so unhappy, in fact, that he became very ill. But
his mother was courageous and determined, and
would not give her boy up. Fortunately the
Czar of Russia was her friend, and at last King
Milan was deposed, and Queen Natalie allowed
to return and live with her boy again. He is now
the boy king of his small country, but it is his
Ministers who rule for him. And as I look at
this last picture of him I see his face has grown
much graver and older than it was when I used
to see it in Florence, and there is a look in his
dark eyes which makes me wonder if he does
not talk very thoughtfully to his beautiful mother
sometimes, and ask her if she can tell him how a
boy can best learn to be a king.

The other little prince—who, dressed in a white
frock, rests his baby head against his mother's
cheek, and clings to her with tiny hands—is not
really a prince, after all, but a King—a poor, innocent baby King, with no one to protect him
but his brave young mother.

I am never happy about him. I am always

sorry for him. He touches me to the very heart. He is the little king of Spain. He never saw his father—he was born after his death. Poor baby, born with the weight of a crown upon his head. And it is not a light weight to bear in Spain. Its wearer has to govern a passionate, tumultuous, rebellious people, divided amongst themselves, subtle and clever at intrigue and plot, who would not be sorry for the five-year-old baby, who, if he is strong enough to grow up to be a young man, will be called upon to face and to try to control all this. And he is not a strong little prince. He has always been delicate, and not very long ago was so ill that everyone thought he would die; and one can imagine the suffering of those days for the poor mother watching over his bed, soothing his pain, kissing his poor little hot forehead, and praying only that her baby might be well again and smile at her once more, while she knew that the grand, clever Court Ministers were only waiting to see whether the King would live or die. I think sometimes she must have longed to snatch him away from all those watching eyes, and carry him into some pretty room where she could hold him in her arms and rock him to sleep all by herself, and talk soft, coaxing, soothing nonsense to him, and never let him hear anyone say, " Your Majesty."

I knew a bright, clever American woman who

had seen this little King often under very interesting circumstances.

There are not many people—even Spaniards—who see him in the same way. She had talked to him and shown him pictures, and she told me some very pretty stories about him. Somehow it rather touched me when she described this white-frocked baby's entrance into a room, and his holding out his tiny hand to be kissed, and her playful talk with him in which she addressed him always as " Your Majesty." It would have seemed so much more natural to have picked him up in one's arms and kissed him on his soft cheeks and on his soft neck, and to have held him on one's knee and played with him. But of course it would be very improper to romp with a King, and especially a King of Spain.

But there is one thing that even Kings and Princes cannot be deprived of even by etiquette —that is a mother. All the eight I write of have as much luxury of that sort as if they were not Royal at all. And this little King of Spain has one of the tenderest, and wisest, and sweetest. She lives only to guard and love and care for this helpless little King. She is young and fair, and a Queen, but she does not care for the world. She is so brave, and so gentle, and so wise, that even her enemies and her baby's foes have learned to respect her and know that she is not to be trifled with. It is said that even the gentlest, most timid creature will be brave when its little ones are in danger—even a soft-eyed deer will stand at bay. This young Queen Mother is brave like that, and I think that everyone with a kind heart watches her with interest, and hopes that her sweet courage and faithfulness will be rewarded, and her boy will live to wear his crown through a long life, and be the best King that Spain has ever known.

The eighth Prince is not a little one now. He is twenty or twenty-one years old, but I think of him as still a boy, because I have usually seen his boy pictures. He is the Prince Royal of Italy, and his name is Victor Emanuel—Vittorio Emmanuele in Italian. After all I think it is his beautiful mother, Queen Margherita, who gives me my interest in him. In the Italian cities one sees so many pictures of her with the ropes of her famous pearls wound round and round her throat. She has made herself so beloved by the people, because she is so sweet, and also, I have no doubt, because she has been such a good mother, and has loved her one boy so dearly.

I was at Milan a few months ago, and I drove out to Monza, which is one of the Royal summer villas. It is a drive of about two hours from Milan, and the afternoon was one I shall not forget. It was early spring in Italy, and the long winding drive through the beautiful park where troops of little fawns and quite unalarmed deer made their way through the young trees and long grass, looking back at us with soft wonder, was a lovely thing to remember. The ground was yellow with countless myriads of primroses, and the air was sweet with the breath of as many violets. I stopped the carriage more than once, and we got out and filled the drapery of our dresses with the pale yellow and deep blue blossoms—enough to fill our rooms in the hotel to overflowing.

The King and Queen were in Rome, and the Villa was open to visitors. So we went through it—through all the beautiful saloons and the rest. And it was in the Queen's bedroom that I was assured that this Prince at least must have been a happy one—as happy as love could make him. There were pictures of him everywhere. His was the principal picture that hung on the walls. He must have had his portrait painted every year since he was born. When Queen Margherita opens her beautiful eyes in the morning she sees him at all ages. As a baby in a long lace frock, as a baby in a short one, as a tiny boy, as a bigger one. He is represented from stage to stage until he stands in his uniform a schoolboy prince. That pretty sumptuous room—the bedroom of a queen with all those pictures of a boy

—loved every year from his babyhood with that love which makes every mother a queen and every queen only a sweet woman—that pretty bedroom told its own story of a happy prince who may be a good king.

These are the eight Princes I feel as if I know though they do not know me, and even in the most republican country in the world—even in America which does not believe in kings—I am sure there is no one who will not say in thinking of these boys, "God keep the little princes and help them to care for their people, and God bless the queens who are their mothers."

ONE WHO LIVED LONG, LONG AGO

ONE WHO LIVED LONG, LONG AGO

IT would be very difficult to tell anything at all definite about her. One can only try to imagine what she was like, what she thought, what she did, and how her young life was passed. And imagination, however powerful, can scarcely be relied on to depict to one very clearly and truly the things that happened more than 1800 years ago.

More than 1800 years ago she died in the ancient city of Pompeii, an awful tragic death, which 2000 people shared with her, perishing in the most overwhelming catastrophe the world has ever known. And yet to-day one can pass through the streets she walked about in, standing in the " peristylium " or court of the house which was, perhaps, the one she lived in, and where her favorite flowers grew; and where she amused herself by watching the goldfishes in the little oblong stone-lined pool, which we are told was called the Piscina. One sees, perhaps, her very own little bedroom, where she slept with her playthings about her, as rosy and peaceful as other little girls sleep to-day in their bedrooms in London or New York. And one can stand and look down pityingly at the slender lava and ash-encrusted little form, which was all that the great eruption of Mount Vesuvius on the 24th of August, A.D. 79, left of her childish body. She is lying by her mother, just as she fell when they were trying to escape among the blinding showers of hot ashes, red-hot lapilli, or small fragments of pumice-stone, and the sudden deluge of boiling water, which the great volcano poured forth alternately, and sometimes all at once, and which turned the beautiful day into black night, filled the air with shrieks of terror, and the narrow streets with bewildered, agonized people losing their way and stumbling in the horrible darkness as they were flying for their lives.

Many hundred years she lay in the darkness with the gay, luxurious little city she had lived in, and which the quaking earth had broken into ruins and the burning mountain had covered with shower after shower of lapilli and ashes until it was buried twenty feet deep, no trace of it left to show that it had ever existed.

When one stands in the small museum and looks down at the slender, lava-encrusted frame, which looks more like a curiously-rough gray image than anything else, it is difficult to think of it as the body of a real, living young creature, warm and soft, and full of movement and color. And yet she was so—eighteen hundred and eleven years ago.

If she had died as others do, she would have been dust centuries ago, but as it is, she lies in the tiny Pompeii museum, in a glass case, near that other lava-encrusted image which is supposed to have been her mother, and with other like images near her, and one stands and looks at her with thrilled wonder, and tries to imagine what she looked like, what her short life was, and if all was quickly over when she fell, amid the stifling ashes, the sulphurous vapor, the sudden unnatural gusts of hot wind, the flashes of ghastly lightning, and the awful volcano's thunder.

In a case near her there is a poor dog with what seems to have been quite a beautiful collar round his neck. He is lying in a distorted position on his back, his feet in the air, and his mouth open as if he had died on giving a last yelp of terror and pain. I wondered if perhaps he had been her dog, and I hoped he was not, or that she had not heard his poor cry for the help which she could not give.

It was her figure which was my companion all the soft sunny day as I wandered through the once brilliant little city where she had lived and died. My friends did not see her, but I did, and fancied even that I felt the touch of her little hand. No one could hear her, for she moved so softly. But when I imagined that she walked with me, she was no longer a poor little gray lava-encrusted thing, but supple and pretty and soft, and clothed in the delicate, graceful garments she wore so long ago—or at least as nearly as my imagination, assisted by Alma Tadema's beautiful pictures, could array her.

But for those wonderful pictures I think I could not have really called her to life, but remembering them I made a little shadow which seemed almost more than a shadow—a slender figure, in a graceful little white tunic falling in simple, lovely folds, and with a border of gold or purple, or purple and gold together. She had small sandals on her slim feet, and a light wreath of flowers on her delicate head. As for her face, I only seemed to see that it was sweet and innocent and fair, that there was a childish rose bloom on her cheeks, that her eyes were deep and shadowy under their long lashes, and that she had blue-black hair, which was not long, but waved softly about her head and neck, and shaded her forehead a little, as it might if she lived in the present day.

She was my guide, and she seemed to tell me many things and make the dead ancient city live again, though I do not know how I understood her, for I think she used to speak Latin when she was alive. But there was a guide in uniform who led our party, and as he explained things in French, perhaps I stole the words from him and altered them, and added to them, and translated them into the music of the voice that ceased speaking one thousand eight hundred and eleven years ago.

I have many interesting days in my life to remember, but among them all there is not one which stands out as a memory so utterly, strangely beautiful and absorbing as that day spent rambling through the streets and ruins of a long, long dead city warmly flooded with an Italian sun. It must have been such a gay and brilliant little place, with its richly colored and decorated houses, their flower-wreathed red or yellow columns, their bright courtyards, their fountains and vines, the graceful temples and theatres and villas, the great mountain behind, the blue Mediterranean at its feet.

"It was very beautiful," I thought my little shadow told me. "The people were so gay and rich. It was not so stately and magnificent as Rome, but it was so bright and luxurious. There were so many flowers everywhere, the sky was always so blue and the sun so warm. We lived so much out of doors, we used to sit and work and take our meals in the open court, and the wine cups were wreathed with flowers, and garlands hung from the columns and were twined about them, and we wore fresh garlands on our heads—every one wore them when there was gayety and feasting."

"You were never afraid of the great mountain then," I said, and I looked up at it as it towered so near us, dark and bare-looking and sullen with its cloud of smoke rolling upward and about its summit.

"No one was afraid of it then—particularly not the children. We used to hear that, years before—when some of us were not born—there had been a great earthquake which the mountain had caused, but it seemed so quiet and peaceful, covered with beautiful meadows, and the earthquake seemed to us to have been so long ago, that it would have seemed only like a legend if we had not been able to see some of the ruins it had made, and the Forum which was being rebuilt. It was not finished when the great eruption came, which burned everything. ' When you go into it to-day, you will see the unfinished columns just as the slaves left them when they turned and fled into the darkness to try to save their lives."

And then there came to my mind a paragraph I remembered reading in Bulwer's " Last Days of Pompeii."

" At one of the public edifices appropriated to

the business of the city, workmen were employed
upon the columns, and you heard the noise of
their labor every now and then, rising above the
hum of the multitude. The columns are unfinished to this day."

We went into the ruins of the Forum—the
great mart and gathering place of those ancient
days—and saw the rows of incompleted pillars,
standing still. To one who was not told their
story they would look as if they had all been
broken smoothly off at about the same height.

"It was very busy and gay here once," my
small shadow seemed to tell me. "There were
such crowds of people coming and going. They
came to meet each other if they were rich and
idle, to do all sorts of business, to buy and sell,
to saunter and look on, to sit and eat and drink
and talk over all that happened. The magistrates
decided cases here. There was the Temple of
Jupiter, where the Senators met. The garments
worn were so graceful and so rich. There was
so much purple and gold and ornament. The
clasps and girdles of the rich ones sparkled with
jewels, and they wore such splendid rings and
chains. There was so much luxury and pleasure
and the people seemed to enjoy themselves so.
This place used to seem like a great brilliant
fair."

One hears so much of the past luxuries and

splendors of this small dead city that in visiting it one wonders continually how this luxury exhibited itself. The streets are so very narrow that an ordinary modern carriage could not pass through them. In the days when people drove through the narrow streets two-wheeled chariots were used—one sees to-day the deep grooves worn by the wheels into the stone of the pavement ; we are told that there were numbers of such chariots, and that they were very elegant and elaborate in their artistic decoration, but how it would be possible for two to pass each other, when the worn grooves seem to prove there was barely room for the wheels of one, is a mystery which appears unexplained. Our guide could not tell us, and as he could not I could not imagine the answer my shadow might have given.

And yet we are told that the streets were brilliant once — that they were filled with richly-attired people, jewelled and clad in Tyrian dyes ; that beautiful women, gracefully veiled, passed through them followed by slaves, that the shops glittered with wonderful and beautiful things, that one caught glimpses of fountains and exquisite temples and triumphal arches, that all was brightness and grace and color and wealth of life. To-day one only sees the narrow streets, the broken columns, the fallen temples and the ruins of the houses that were their owners' tombs 1800 years ago.

Though my shadow companion could not make me understand what her answers might have been to some of the questions I should have liked to ask, and which neither my imagination nor the uniformed guide could reply to, yet I think her presence helped me to give some fancied life and color to the ruined houses, and make them something as they might have been when they were homes.

Through street after narrow street we walked, through houses and temples, through forums and once sumptuous baths and theatres. The excavations which are made by the government are still going on. The silent streets, the ruins themselves seem to be kept swept and in order. But for the broken halls and columns, the roofless buildings left open to the sunshine, all is so free from obstacles and rubbish that one says to one's self again and again, " Eighteen centuries ! eighteen centuries since Pompeiian feet trod these stones."

The large streets are called " Strada," the smaller ones " Vicolo." The Strada di Mercurio (the Street of Mercury), the Strada della Fortuna (the Street of Fortune), the Strada dell' Abbondanza (the Street of Abundance), the Strada delle Terme (Street of the Baths), Strada del

Foro (Street of the Forum), the Vicolo del Fauno (Little Street of the Faun), Vicolo del Balcone Pensile (Street of the Hanging Balcony).

These are of course only a few of the names. All the houses have their names also, most of them taken from some statue or painting which decorated them. Some of them were given by the scientific excavators, and were taken from seal or signet ring found in the ruins.

There is the Casa di Apollo (House of Apollo), the House of Adonis, the House of Castor and Pollux, the House of the Faun, the House of the Little Fountain, and of the Great Fountain, the House of the Tragic Poet, the House of Pansa, the House of Sallust, the House of the Centaur. They are all names like these.

In the present day when a man builds a house he builds it solely after his own tastes and fancies. His entrance hall is square, or oblong, or irregular, as he pleases ; he builds as many stories as he is inclined to mount ; he places his dining-room, his bedroom, and library, just where he thinks best. In other times there seems to have been an idea that the houses men lived in should naturally be as much alike as the shells on the backs of snails and tortoises are like each other. In London one sees rows and rows of melancholy struct-ures all exactly the same ; one sees them in New York, though there they are not smoke-begrimed

all to one hopelessly dingy shade. And in Pom
peii one passes from street to street and finds in
all the houses the one plan.

One enters through a narrow passage the "vestibulum," which leads one to a court, which was
called "atrium," and which has in the centre a
sort of square, shallow pool made in the mosaic
pavement to receive the rain water which emptied itself into it from the aperture in the sloping
roof. This was called the "impluvium." At the
opposite end of this "atrium" was a room called
the "tablinum," and all around it tiny rooms
which, in modern days, would seem scarcely
more than closets. But it was the centre court
or "peristylium," where the people really lived,
and which I am sure they must have felt to be
truly their home. Surely they could not have
spent much time in the tiny rooms, which had
no windows, and no doors to close—only draperies to hang over them.

But the "peristyle" was open to the sunshine
and the blue Southern Italian sky. There was a
colonnade around it, whose columns were gar-
landed with flowers. The centre was a garden.
There was the tiny piscina with the goldfish;
there were pedestals with vases of brilliant flowers upon them; perhaps there was a fountain,
and sometimes a graceful statue.

Around this peristyle there were other tiny

rooms in which the people of the house must have slept. They used to sit in the shade of the colonnade and work or receive their guests there.

I tried to imagine one of these houses as it was when my little shadow, with the blue-black hair and deep soft eyes, and the white tunic, played in the peristylium. I tried to make a picture of the red and yellow columns, the gay colors, the frescoes, the rich draperies, the mosaic pavements, the graceful couches of bronze ornamented with gold and silver, the wonderful sumptuous stuffs thrown over them. But though with the help of what I had heard and read and seen I could make a sort of half antique Roman, half antique Grecian picture, I could not find in it very definite surroundings for my little girl. What did children do eighteen hundred years ago? Does any one really know? I think there were no antique Pompeiian dolls excavated. I saw none in the museum. But surely she had something of wood or stone or some composition, which was made in the form of a miniature child, and which she could hold in her arms and sing to sleep, and dress when it awakened, in a doll's tunic and sandals and girdle, and for whose head she could twine a tiny garland of flowers. Ah! it must have been so even eighteen hundred and eleven years ago.

She had no books to read; even the grown-up

people had scarcely any. "A very small room," we are told, "was sufficient to contain the few rolls of papyrus which the ancients deemed a notable collection of books." She must have looked at the frescoes on the walls, the pictured legends of gods and goddesses, and told herself stories about them. Perhaps her mother told her about them, too, and perhaps there was some favorite slave — a sort of Pompeiian Uncle Remus — who could tell stories of goddesses and gods, of Fauns and Satyrs, and of his own country, from which he had, perhaps, been taken as a prisoner of war.

For the rest she had the flowers and the gold-fish, it may be, some birds, or a pet dog with a golden collar.

"There was a beautiful sea, too," I fancied her saying. "It was as blue as the sky, and there were ships coming and going from strange countries. And we loved the mountain then. It was beautiful, too. It was covered with lovely soft green meadows, and the most fertile vineyards were upon it. The grapes in them were larger and more purple and sweeter than those that grew anywhere else. Only at the very top it was sterile, and the earth was like ashes, and the rocks were blackened as if they had been burned. Wise men who had climbed to look at them used to say strange things about them, and tell strange stories. They said that it might once have been a volcano, one of the mountains that are filled with fire, and which sometimes spout forth flames and showers of boiling water and molten stones. They were stories which made me afraid, but I could not help drawing near to listen when they talked; but I did not believe that there ever had been a time when our beautiful green mountain had been so terrible. The children used to talk about it among themselves, and speak of the soft grass and the flowers that grew on it, and the sweet purple and white grapes in the vineyards, and say it must be all a philosopher's legend, and could not be true."

We went to the wonderful baths where the rich and idle spent the greater part of their days lounging, talking, listening to the reading of some poet, and passing under the hands of slaves —through the luxurious processes of bathing. We saw the public fountains at the ends of the streets, with the grooves worn away in the stone by the many hands and vessels which had rested there when water was drawn. We explored the Temples of the gods—of Apollo, of Mercury, of Jupiter, of Hercules, of Venus, of Fortune, and the Temple of the Egyptian goddess Isis, through the lips of whose image an oracle was believed to speak.

"People used to come here," explained my

shadow, "to ask if their voyages and ventures and other affairs would be successful. It was very wonderful to hear Isis give them the answers."

It must have seemed very wonderful then, but it does not seem so wonderful to-day when one is shown the secret staircase which was found among the excavations—and which was the means the priests used to make their way to the place behind the goddess, from where their voices would seem to come from her oracular lips.

"But none of the gods prophesied what was coming on that terrible day," I said. "There was no warning."

We had walked for hours through the narrow, sunny, silent streets, we had sat on the steps of altars of the ruined temples, we had stood in the amphitheatre where the gladiators fought with wild beasts and with each other, and where the blood of criminals and martyrs flowed upon the sands of the arena amid the applause of these strange people, to whom the agonies of despair and death were an amusement.

All the day I felt the presence of the mountain brooding over us and the ruins it had made. It seemed such an awful, sullen, mysterious power. Who could tell what it might do at any moment? Silent and calm for centuries, the very cattle at one time browsing on its crater, who could have feared it? Luxurious little cities had clustered at its feet, homes and happiness and pleasure had grown beneath its soft smiling shadow. But here one stranger from a far-away country sat wondering and dreaming on the steps of the altars of the Temple of Venus in the ruins of Pompeii.

As I tried to imagine that strange, awful last day, I tried also to make quite real my little slender shadow with the blue-black hair; I wanted to know what she had thought and felt. Poor little shadow with the innocent face smiling under her light wreath of flowers.

"And there was no warning," I kept thinking. And this is what my imagination made her tell me.

"No, there was no warning. At least there was none we could understand and feel real fear of. We were so sure of our Vesuvius. We had never doubted it. For some days before, the weather was very hot—but it was often hot. And there were heavy curious clouds hovering about the mountain top—but though we watched them and spoke to each other about them we were not afraid. Clouds always gathered there when there were storms. But it was very hot and the air seemed so close and heavy. The morning of that last day, I felt languid when I awoke, and I went

"I SMOOTHED ITS FEATHERS SOFTLY"

into the peristyle to see if it would be cooler.
But it seemed even hotter there. The garlands
were drooping and the flowers hung their heads.
They looked so tired and thirsty that I gave
them some water. And as I went from one to
the other, I saw that the goldfish in the ' piscina '
looked tired too. I went and looked at them.
They were so still that at first I was almost afraid
they might be dead. They scarcely moved at
all, and seemed sometimes to gasp for breath.
While I was watching them something flew past
me and alighted at my feet. It came so close
that I could scarcely believe it was a bird. But
it was one—a pretty little bird which seemed to
have fallen frightened and exhausted. Its feathers were ruffled, and it was panting for breath
and held its tiny beak open. It looked at me with
such timid bright eyes as if it wanted me to be
kind and protect it. I think it must have flown
from the mountain and felt the first stifling vapors. But I did not think of that then. It let
me stoop down and take it in my hand gently.
It nestled down in my palm as if it felt comforted
a little. I smoothed its feathers softly and gave
it some water. It drank but it would not eat,
and all the time it looked at me with its timid
bright eyes as if it were asking me a question. I
did not try to keep it prisoner, but it would not
leave me. It seemed to like best to be in my

hand. It was with me to the last. I think all the animals were frightened and felt that something terrible was near. My little dog was restless and turned round and round on his bed as if he were afraid to lie down, and again and again he lifted his head and gave long doleful howls.

"The day got hotter and hotter. I tried to sleep in the shade of the colonnade, and the little bird nestled in the folds of my tunic on my breast. But we neither of us slept, and it kept ruffling its feathers and opening its beak as if to get the air.

"And the flowers drooped so that at last I thought I would give them more water to drink. I gave them all some and went to look at the goldfish again. I was standing near them when suddenly I heard a strange rumbling sound, and felt myself shaken as if the earth were trembling; the fish were darting to and fro, the water in their basin was agitated, my little dog ran cowering to me, and the bird fluttered wildly about my head. I knew what earthquakes were, and I guessed this was one and turned to run to find my mother. But in a moment there were awful sounds on every side. There was the crash of falling walls, and roofs and pillars, and a great darkness seemed to come from the mountain— a blackness lighted with deep burning red. I looked up where the strange clouds had been hovering, and there was a great tree of fire flaming to the skies. Its trunk was blackness, but its branches were flame. Then an awful volume of the blackness rolled over us and seemed to swallow the city up. I ran screaming to my mother's rooms. She met me before I reached them, and caught my hand in the darkness, and we ran through the falling vestibulum into the street. It was filled with shrieking, flying people. On all sides things were falling, the air was filled with stifling vapors, and we were smothered with heavy showers of hot ashes and scorched with burning fragments of pumice stone. We could not see and we could not breathe; I could scarcely cry out when a house or a temple crumbled near me, or a huge red-hot boulder came flying from the awful mountain and fell at my feet.

" We ran hither and thither in the darkness, not knowing where to go; we stumbled over crushed and dead bodies, the ashes and lapilli came thicker and thicker. And in the midst of it I had a strange thought of the beautiful peristylium, with the garlands and statues and flowers, and the goldfish in the little crystal pool.

" I do not know how long we ran and struggled over the ruins in our way. It could not have been long, because the ashes came so thickly, and there was no air to breathe, but it seemed as if we ran to and fro for hours. Then there came more awful sounds from the mountain, more flames, more ashes, more stone, and what seemed a scalding rain. Boiling water was spouting forth with all the rest, and mixed with the ashes and molten stones, it fell upon us. I could run no more, and fell writhing on the trembling earth. My mother would not leave me. She struggled to raise me and then fell too. I only remember one thing more — that I thought how soft and green the mountain had been only the day before — that I remembered the garlands again, and the thirsty flowers and frightened goldfish, and I wondered where the little bird had gone."

This was what I imagined she told me in the voice and language of a little girl of to-day. One can imagine anything and make it seem real to oneself—even the story of a poor little gray image in a glass case—all that awful Last Day left to the child who had died in Pompeii eighteen hundred and eleven years ago.

THE LITTLE FAUN

THE LITTLE FAUN

THE boys and girls who have seen many pictures will be sure to have seen somewhere the picture of a Faun. To those who have not chanced to see one I will explain that a Faun is a strange, beautiful, mythical creature, half a human being, half a happy, lawless, wild-woodland thing. No one ever really saw a Faun except on canvas or in marble, but he is generally represented with a laughing, roguish face, slightly pointed ears, and a quite unclothed body, the lower half of which is like that of some slender wild animal, being covered with shaggy hair, and having beautiful hoofs instead of feet. This figure of the imagination belongs to the old classic days, when gods and goddesses were supposed to roam about the world, and have all sorts of romantic adventure, such as one may read of in Lemprière's Classical Dictionary, which, by the way, I adored when I was a little girl at school, and which I used to keep in a convenient corner of my desk, so that I could dip into it and snatch a legend while I was looking for pencils or geographies. The Faun is supposed to be a sort of wild, happy god of woodland life and joys. At least that is, I think, the easiest way to describe it. As there were woodland nymphs who were called Dryads, and water nymphs who were called Naïads, so there were Fauns. There were in the old stories imaginary creatures who were called Satyrs, but I think in them there was generally supposed to be evil and ungentleness. It is a difficult matter to be definite in describing the character of things living only in fancy, and legends, and pictures—but the Fauns of my imaginings were as free from evil as they were from thoughts; they lived as their friends the trees and little wild living things did, they were happy in the warm sunshine, in the cool rain, in the softness of the thick, green moss, in the damp fragrance of the earth and leaves after a storm ; the rushing wind pleased them, the patter of the raindrops on the trees, the swaying of the branches and the bending of the grass, the light, the green dimness of the forest's shadow, the sounds of the birds going to sleep or awakening, the ferns, the bushes. Everything that lived and grew and was part of Nature was part of the Fauns too, and gave them their wild, careless, half-human, half-animal joy. I have always thought that it must have been a happy thing to be a Faun, and I have amused myself by imagining that, perhaps, in those old

classic days, the legends were true, and that great
light happiness, which fills all one's mind and
body in the spring when the earth is awakening
and breathing the odor of greenness and freshness of things growing—comes to us from some
of those Fauns and Dryads of ages ago, and perhaps we are a little like them sometimes yet.
And I have even pleased myself by thinking I
saw in young human things all joyous at being
alive, a something a little like that old joyousness
of nature in a troop of young Fauns. There is a
buoyant, laughing young Faun who goes with me
everywhere; I think there is also one I see every
day playing in all sorts of weathers, in the one
street of the tiny German village among the hills
and pine forests where I am staying now. But
the one I am going to tell you about did not live
among mountains and forests and wild straw-
berries and flowers and tumbling streams—he
lived in a small house in a Washington Street,
and I think his mother was a dressmaker.

Poor, beautiful, happy little Faun. I did not
know his name, and I could see no reason for his
being happy at all, and yet I never saw anything
so perfectly full of joy from morning until night.

Washington has been growing into a very
beautiful city during the last ten years, but when
I first went to live there it had one great peculi-
arity. In almost every nice wide street one saw

small shabby cottages or tumble-down shanties side by side with the largest and most comfortable houses there were to be found in the city. The effect was not so beautiful as it was droll, but sometimes it was the means of showing one contrasts in life.

The house in which I lived then belonged to General Grant, it having been presented to him by some of his friends and admirers. At the corner of the same side of the street was a large brick house where General Garfield lived; opposite my house there was a small row of frame houses all occupied by colored people, and opposite General Garfield's corner was the small brick house inhabited by the dressmaker whose little boy was a Faun.

I never saw the dressmaker, I only heard somehow that she existed, and that she was the little Faun's mother.

I think she must have been a poor dressmaker. Perhaps she used to sit upstairs in some back room and cut out patterns and sew very hard; at least that is the picture I always made of her when I watched the darling little Faun, and wondered why he was uncared-for and always alone. I felt sure she must love him, and would have washed and dressed ·him if she had had time.

Only a few yards from my front door were two

A LITTLE FAUN

beautiful, thick-leaved, full-branched maple trees. When regular rows of trees were being planted in the streets, General Grant saved the lives of these two, which were to have been cut down. They were such beautiful trees. They shaded all the house, and were so intimate with me, that each spring they sent out longer and longer shoots from their branches, until Boy and the Socialist — who were tiny fellows then — could stand at the nursery windows and shake hands with them.

These sociable branches were most friendly at the nursery windows, and the windows of my workroom on the third story. The workroom was called The Den, and it was a very pretty room, and its windows looked in the most familiar manner into the very nests of the bird families who built on the tops of the two trees.

I was very intimate with the birds—quite on visiting terms. They used to perch on my window ledge sometimes and talk to each other about me, and they quarrelled with each other without the slightest embarrassment as they hopped about the branches. There was a lady sparrow who lived in a most fashionable nest at the very top, and who used to scold her husband severely and chirp back at him like a vixen when he dared to answer her. I think she used to accuse him of bringing indigestible worms to his family, and say that a sparrow with the least proper domestic feeling would provide more carefully.

I used to hold my pen still to listen and watch. I was always listening and watching those two, and it was while being idle like that one day that I caught my first glimpse of the little Faun. For a moment I lowered my eyes to a part of the streets below; I could see through the branches, and there was the tiny Faun dancing on the pavement before his own small front door. I did not know he was a Faun then—I only thought of that afterwards when I had seen him oftener, and knew more of his bright gleeful ways. At that moment I only saw the most beautiful, unwashed, half-clothed little creature one could imagine. He was perhaps four or five years old; he had no hat and no shoes or stockings, indeed he had on nothing but a fluttering little calico slip. Fortunately it was a warm day in the early summer, and besides, being a Faun, I dare say he would not have been happy in ordinary clothes. His way of dancing was simply to hop lightly from one foot to the other, and sometimes turn round, keeping time to the music of his own pretty laughs. As he danced, his dingy calico slip fluttered about, and I could see his round bare limbs on which he wore nothing at all. I saw him every day for several weeks, and I never saw him with any more clothes on; and I do not think I ever knew

his curly hair to be brushed, though sometimes—
very rarely—I suspected he had been caught and
washed. But his hair was so curly that perhaps
it might have been brushed without one's knowing it. It was such pretty hair, not long, but such
a bright color, and all one mass of soft curls and
rings which danced as he danced. As for his
face, it was the roundest, dimpled, lovely laughing one. It looked as if it knew of nothing else
but laughing. That is one reason I always
thought his mother must have loved him, even
though she was too busy to take much care of
him. If she had not loved him, he would not always have been so gay.

But he was always gay. I became as accustomed to watching him as I was to watching the
bird families in my trees, indeed, I think I began
to watch the birds less whenever the little Faun
was to be seen.

He did not seem to play with other children.
He was always by himself, always wore the one
small calico garment, and was always enjoying
himself. I do not remember ever having seen him
stand quite still. He was nearly always dancing
from one foot to the other, and talking and laughing to himself. I have seen him run out into the
street when it rained, and dance about with the
rain-drops falling on his curls, just as I am sure
the young Fauns must have done in their for-

ests after the hot days. He liked the rain as he liked the sunshine, and I dare say each drop on his cheeks or his curls seemed like a little kiss.

I am sure he had no toys, and I fancy he did not think of wanting them. He used to amuse himself sometimes with leaves and pebbles, and bits of grass. Perhaps he was more intimate than I was with the birds in the maples, and when they perched on the dressmaker's fence and twittered, they were telling him interesting things only a little Faun would understand, and which I was too stupid and human to comprehend. Who knows but that they told him stories of birds who knew other birds who had been in strange, mythical countries, where there were forest glades where Fauns hid themselves still? At least it is certain he was never at a loss for amusement, and never tired of talking to the sunshine and the summer wind, and the rain-drops, and the leaves. Once quite an ordinary adventure befell him, but I am sure he not only did not mind it at all, but he enjoyed it very much.

Perhaps he had been listening to the birds' stories, and had thought he could dance happily away, and find the other little Fauns in the deep, shadowy forest glades. At any rate he strayed away and was lost. I don't know where he went. I only knew he had been lost when I looked out through the branches and saw the big policeman bringing him home.

The big policeman was the one whose " beat " took in our street. I did not really quite know him to speak to myself, but I *almost* knew him because Boy and the Socialist were really on intimate terms with him. Boy and the Socialist were so little then that they wore short white kilts and large sashes, and socks, and long curly hair, and it was considered a most splendid and daring social feat to know and actually talk to a policeman. In fact I believe this policeman was not at all ferocious, and that he even liked beautiful little boys who regarded him with admiration. But it was very grand to know him well enough to look through the iron fence and say, " Halloa, Mr. Niel; good morning!" when he walked slowly past, and even on occasions to saunter out and stride manfully by his side, engaged in sprightly conversation, the short, plump legs in white socks doing their best to keep up with the big, long ones, and having to accomplish it by trotting.

Boy and the Socialist always spoke of him reverentially as " Mr. Niel," and said he was " such a nice colored gentleman. He talks to us just as if he wasn't a policeman at all." He even condescended to let them examine his club, and I seem to have some recollection of their having discovered that it was true that he sometimes carried a pistol. It was this "nice colored gentleman" who found the Faun and brought him home. I saw them crossing the street together. Mr. Niel was very big and muscular, and could have managed a burglar or a riotous person very easily; but the Faun had evidently not a shadow of anything but friendly pleasure in his society. He was holding Mr. Niel's hand and dancing along by his side, from one foot to another, as he always did. His curly hair was golden in the sun, he was as dirty as a little Faun could be, but he was laughing and talking as he hopped, and Mr. Niel was laughing too. It was not such a small thing as being lost in a big city and brought home in the custody of a big policeman, that would disturb or frighten a little Faun. He had played with lions and leopards in his forests in those long-past ages when he had been a real Faun, and he was not likely to be afraid of a policeman.

I do not know exactly how it was we never had any opportunity of knowing the little Faun any better. Perhaps it was because of his habit of amusing himself and not caring much for the society of others. But once I held him in my arms for a few minutes, and Boy and the Socialist played with him.

We were just on the point of going away to the seaside, and as the weather was becoming warm

I used sometimes to sit out of doors under the maples in the evening while Boy and the Socialist played on the tiny square of grass before the drawing-room windows.

We were there together one evening when I saw the little Faun coming slowly across the street toward us. He was not dancing as usual, though he made occasional little hops as he drew near, watching us with a sort of wistful look in his eyes. Perhaps it was because as it was such a warm evening he thought it looked cool and pleasant under the trees where the mamma, in a thin white frock, watched the two little fellows who had such bright hair and bright sashes, and who were all in white, too.

I think that must have been it. He was as unwashed as usual himself, and his pretty curls were all tangled, and he had evidently worn his one little garment several days. But he did not mind that, of course, and I am sure it never came into his mind that there was any difference between the two pretty boys and his own pretty self. They were romping, happy Fauns too, notwithstanding their embroidered frocks and white sashes.

I watched him as he came closer and closer, just as some dear little animal in the woods might come toward things he liked to look at. I did not say anything at first because I was afraid of startling him, and making him run away as a squirrel or rabbit might.

But by the time he had reached the gate and taken hold of it and was looking through, Boy and the Socialist saw him, and stopped their playing to look at him.

It was just as if three large-eyed, sociable, little woodland creatures had met. They drew near to each other, the two pairs of brown eyes fixed on the one pair of blue ones, with a soft, friendly curiosity. As for me, I kept quite still and watched. I wanted so much to see how little Fauns made friends.

I do not to this day know quite how it was done. There certainly was not a shadow of ceremony. In a few moments the gate was opened and there were some pretty joyous sounds, and three little Fauns were jumping and laughing together as if they had played in the same forest since they were born.

How they enjoyed themselves, and how pleased the two clean little Fauns were with the dirty one. I am sure they thought it an accomplishment to be able to have such a dirty face and such tangled hair, though indeed they were extremely talented themselves in that direction. But they shouted and jumped about, and rolled on the square of grass, and tumbled over each other. They cared no more about their frocks and sashes than young birds care about their feathers.

But in the midst of their pleasure an accident happened. They had always been under the impression that the iron fence had been invented and put round the grass simply that they might have something to climb on, in fact they believed that everything that could be climbed on or over was made expressly for them. So of course they began to climb manfully, and their new friend climbed too, and somehow he lost his hold and fell.

I dare say the little Fauns of classic days did not hurt themselves when they fell, and so they never cried, but this poor little man got a very hard bump and he broke out into quite a splendid roar. I sprang from my seat and ran to him and picked him up in my arms. It was not a serious hurt at all, and I knew the great cure for bumps, so I carried him back to my chair and held him on my knee and petted him, and gave him soft little pats such as I always gave Boy and the Socialist when they were in trouble.

It was then I realized the difference between wild little Fauns and tame ones. My own, too, were so used to be held and patted that when one took them up they nestled down like kittens, but holding this one was like holding a rabbit. He did not seem afraid, and I could see that he liked it, but his small body did not seem to know how to relax itself, and he looked at me through his tears with a sort of wondering gratefulness, as if he were not used to being taken care of in that way. I felt surer than ever that everyone was very busy at his house, and had no time to spare.

But the tears were gone directly. In two minutes he was laughing again and sitting on my knee quite ready for more fun, and the other two were as ready as he.

It occurred to me that perhaps little Fauns were fond of sweet things, and as the dressmaker was poor he might not often taste them; so I took some pennies out of my pocket and put them in his hand.

"Would you like to take those," I said, "and get some candy at the store round the corner?"

He did not say anything—indeed, it is rather curious that I never can remember anything he said, and I tell myself it is perhaps because he spoke only the Faun language, and I did not understand it. But he laughed and looked happy, and the next minute he was out of the gate and dancing across the street.

Boy and the Socialist did not seem surprised that he had left them. Squirrels don't say good bye to each other, and they did not expect that he would be more ceremonious. They began to play together again.

But in a few minutes the little Faun came dancing back. He was all sunshine and smiles, and he had a packet of candy in his hand. He had not even opened it, and I wondered why. I found out directly. He made signs to the two small Fauns inside the gate, and they went towards him. Then he opened his packet, and held it out to them with smiles. They helped themselves cheerfully, and then the little Faun helped himself, and they stood and munched amicably together. You see because he was a Faun he had only sweet, happy, joyous impulses, and did not know what selfishness was, and he did not think of even opening his treasure until he had carried it back to share it with his little fellow-Fauns, even though no one expected for one moment that he would not simply enjoy it by himself.

The next day we went to the seaside, and I never saw my little Faun again. When we returned in the autumn I did not see him dancing before his door for several days, and so I spoke to a servant about him.

"Do you know where the pretty little curly boy is?" I asked. "The one who was always dancing from one leg to the other."

"No, ma'am, I don't," was the answer. "His mother was a dressmaker, and she moved away in the hot weather. I never heard where they went."

I was very sorry. I wanted to know my Faun
better. I felt sure he had a sweet, lovable nature,
and I thought I might do things to please him.
I have never forgotten him, and I often wonder if
he is as happy now that he is a big boy. He
must be a big fellow now. Boy and the Socialist
have had time to grow tall, and travel in foreign
countries, and learn foreign languages, and become enthusiastic electricians and scientists, and
adorers of Edison, but they remember the little
Faun. Some day I think I shall try to write his
story. I wonder if it will be at all like the true
one.

"WHAT USE IS A POET?"

"WHAT USE IS A POET?"

IT was the Socialist who said it, and he said it quite innocently and with a sincere desire for information. The Socialist is always in search of information, and he is always "rising to remark" upon some novel theory or problem.

The most interesting are usually propounded when we are walking together. This particular morning we were walking along a beautiful country road, it being a daily duty he had charged himself with to forcibly relieve me from the sad duties of a sick-room.

It was a very beautiful country road, and the sweet spring air soothed and refreshed me. He looked so rosy and well, and had such coaxing, comforting ways. It seemed as if the shadow of illness or danger could not even approach him.

We walked along, sometimes in the spring sunshine, and the Socialist marched on briskly, sometimes with his hand through my arm, sometimes with his boyish arm round my waist, sometimes with his hands in the pockets of his trim-fitting coat. Socialist though he is, the jaunty close fit of his coat is quite admirable. But this may have something to do with the plump strength of his straight young body.

He seemed to be reflecting for a few minutes. He kept his eyes on the road as he walked, and quite suddenly he asked his question.

" I wish you'd tell me, Chérie, what *is* the use of a poet? What *use* is he?"

It was rather a startling question to me. Limited as my information is on many subjects of vital interest to the Socialist, I try to keep pace with him in such matters as my untrained feminine mind might hope to grasp. And I will say this for him, that he tactfully endeavors to adapt himself to my limitations and not ask me impossible " hard ones." Dynamos he knows I am not equal to, horizontal engines and electric lights he is aware I am not able to grapple with, but poets I might rise to and give reliable opinions about. And, indeed, I always feel it very sweet of him that he gives me nothing much more scientific and complex to explain than mere poets and things of that sort.

And yet the question seemed rather difficult to answer just at first.

" What is the *use* of a poet?" I repeated a little slowly. " What are you thinking of, sweetheart?"

" Well, you see," he answered energetically,

"every man ought to have his *use*. When he does a thing or makes a thing it ought to be useful in some way. When a man makes an engine, or builds a bridge, or invents a telephone, you see what it is for. But what is poetry *for*? What is the *use* of it?"

His rosy cheek looked so round and like a splendid baby's that I could not help smiling and putting a kiss on it as I took his arm.

"You are the Electric boy, aren't you?" I said. "You belong to the telephone age—to the Edison-Bell phonograph steam-heated linotype century."

"Yes, I do," he answered exultantly. "And I am glad of it. But I want to know about poets and poetry. Perhaps it's because I'm only a boy and haven't any genius, but do you know that somehow I can't get interested when I try to read poetry."

"That's all right," I said cheerfully. "Perhaps you will when you are older. There are so many motors to attend to just now."

"Yes," he said. "And it is so easy for a boy to be interested in motors."

"The truth is," I answered, "that this is the Telephone time, and it is tremendously interesting. We are living among such wonderful things, and they are all so useful, that it is quite natural to ask what a thing is 'for.' People in other days used to make journeys to see each other and ask questions, now they can talk through a tube without leaving their rooms; once people kept long-winded diaries, now they can confess into a phonograph; they used to write long business letters, now they cable across the Atlantic, or cross it in a few days, a dozen times a year."

" Yes," said the Socialist, " just think of the fun I have when we go over for the summer, and how different it must have been in the old days. I should almost like to *live* in the engine-room," with rapture.

I am quite aware that he would. The Socialist is a fine product of the Telephone age—and before an engine-room man with a black face—one who could speak with the proper feeling of relationship to boilers and "pressure," pistons and walking beams, the White Czar himself would sink into nonentity.

" It is a beautiful age!" said I.

The Socialist gave me a bright look of scrutiny.

" Are you making fun?" he asked.

" Not at all," I replied. " The wonderful, useful things are of use to everybody in one way or another. They bring the beautiful things to everybody. The poets are better cared for, too. Think what beautiful books their beautiful thoughts are printed in. Think what beautiful pictures often illustrate them. Once great poets

starved and wasted in antechambers, sneered at
by menials, for the coming of the great man who
might give them a few guineas. Great men wait
for poets now, and are pleased to speak with them
of the work they do. The Telephone century
brings the greatest poets and artists, singers and
actors, from one far-off part of the world to the
other, so that everyone can know something of
them."

" That's true, isn't it?" exclaimed the Socialist.
I think he had been a shade anxious lest all the
merits of his beloved dynamos might chance to
fail to be quite appreciated by even a gentle, un-
positive person who was not scientific, and only
could be trusted for definite information on the
subject of poets. But he had been quite safe. It
would never have occurred to me that I could
prove to him the use of poets by decrying what
was so near his heart.

" A book of travels," he explained, " tells you
things. Those papers of Kennan's on Siberia, or
Stanley's ' Darkest Africa '—you get to know so
much when you read them. But what is the use
of writing things in rhyme?"

" I will tell you something," I said. " There
are poets and poets who never wrote a rhyme in
their lives, and who never had a word of their
poems published. And sometimes they have
been the most perfect poets of all."

"Never wrote anything in rhyme?" he exclaimed. "Then how were they poets?"

"I can only tell you my own thoughts about it," I said. "I think a poet is a person who sees things in the most beautiful way, and does things in the most beautiful way, and tells his thoughts in the most beautiful words. Even in the telephone century, you know there are all sorts of troublesome things and tiresome things, and one has often to express things that are difficult. Now if one can say the commonplace or painful things in some sweet or gentle way, one is a sort of poet even though one never dreams of rhyme. It is always easiest and most convincing to illustrate with the things most familiar and near to us. I can illustrate with poor Boy who is so ill. Suppose I were to say to him, 'Yes, you are very ill. You cannot use your cameras, or your engines, or your bicycle any more. You must lie still and take medicine and peptonoids all day and night. When you travel to different countries you will have a doctor and a trained nurse always with you, and your medicine-chest will be in the railway carriage. I shall spend a great deal of money for you, but I don't know when you will get well.' That would be telling him the truth in ugly, hurting words. But if I kneel by him and comfort him, and say, 'Yes, you are ill, darling boy, but it only makes us all feel how much we love you.

And we only live to make the days go easily for you. Everything you would like you shall have. The doctor and the nurse are as nice as they are clever. We will pretend you are the Prince Imperial, and we are your court and have to fly to do your bidding. You shall go to any country you like and that agrees with you, and every country shall give its very nicest things to help and amuse you.' When I tell him the truth in that way he is soothed instead of hurt, and his illness even seems to have a pleasant side."

" Yes, dearest," said the Socialist, holding my arm close.

" And that is what the poet does," I said after a few seconds. " That is the *use* of a poet. When trouble is harsh he tries to find something in it that is gentle; if there is nothing gentle in it, perhaps he is able to tell us how it may teach us courage and patience, and help us to understand the things that hurt others. Then he tells us a great, beautiful truth in such a way that in spite of ourselves we remember it. It may seem a funny thing to say, but there is a very simple ancient poet who is not exactly considered a poet, who will still help me to tell you one thing I mean. Her name was Mother Goose, and she is one of the most celebrated persons in the world. Who do you suppose ever forgets—

> " Little boy blue, come blow your horn,
> The sheep's in the meadow, the cow's in the **corn**.
> Is that the way to mind your sheep,
> Under the haystack fast asleep? "

How the Socialist laughed and hugged my arm!

"No," he said. "Nobody forgets that—even in the telephone century."

"Certainly not," I said. "And why not? I believe it is because of the jingle of the rhyme. I don't think millions of children would have remembered it if it had only been written like this: Blow your trumpet, little boy dressed in blue. You are not minding your sheep. You are fast asleep, and the sheep and cows have got into the corn and the meadow."

"Of course they wouldn't," laughed the Socialist.

"I am certain of it," I answered, laughing too. "And the poets found out that when they put their thoughts into music which was not merely jingle they would somehow return to people's minds because of the melody, and the great thoughts would be remembered and do their work better. Now listen to this. Any boy who thinks and feels can understand it and see that it is splendid and real—

> " Tell me not in mournful numbers
>   Life is but an empty dream,
>   For the soul is dead that slumbers,
>   And things are not what they seem.
>
> " Life is real—life is earnest,
>   And the grave is not its goal;
>   ' Dust thou art, to dust returnest,'
>   Was not spoken of the soul."

" I am not going to repeat a lot of poetry to you, because you will get the most good out of it when you care to read it and think over it for yourself. But that means something, doesn't it? It isn't only rhyming sound."

" Yes, it means something," answered the Socialist, with bright eyes. " Who wrote it?"

" Longfellow. And it is called ' A Psalm of Life.' It is a beautiful thought put into musical words—and you know when you come to think it over, it is as energetic and practical in one way as almost anything in the telephone century. The last verse is full of bravery and force. It goes like this—

> ' Let us then be up and doing,
>   With a heart for any fate,
>   Still achieving, still pursuing,
>   Learn to labor and to wait.'

" An electric boy can comprehend all that. Edison and Bell and the rest have always been 'up and doing.'   Men who make great inventions have to have hearts 'for any fate,' and the more you read of their lives the more you see how they had 'to labor and to wait.'   I dare say some of them have often remembered those lines.   You see that is 'the use of a poet;' his strongest, most beautiful thoughts have something in them that may be a sort of help even for the people whose lives seem all prose.   Perhaps the finest poetry has to be first the reallest prose.   Then it can come home to everybody."

" Well, even I can understand that ' Psalm of Life,' " he said, "and of course I am only a boy."

"Then you know the use of the poet," I said. " And that reminds me of something a great English statesman once said to me about you. He was a very great statesman, whose name is known all over the world.   You know who he was, and that I met him at a lunch party at a villa near Florence."

"Oh, yes, I know," he said. " And I should like to ask him about socialism, but of course he must be too busy to have time for boys."

"He finds time for everything. He sat next to me at lunch, and he said to me, ' What are you doing with the Socialist?'   (Though he did not call you that.) 'What are you letting him learn ? '

" 'Just now,' I answered, 'he is learning French

principally, and as much Italian as he can pick up without a grammar.’

“ ‘ Well,’ he said, ‘ don’t give him too many modern languages.’

“ ‘ But don’t you think they are very useful when a man has his career to make ? ’ I asked.

“ ‘ Yes,’ he replied, ‘ useful. They are excellent tools for work, but a man needs something more than the things that are merely useful. I hold he should be given the ability to understand and appreciate the old classic wonders which will help him to make his mind beautiful and develop its poetic powers. We are too utilitarian in these days. I can’t have any mistakes made in the training of the Socialist. Let him learn his modern languages, but give him the classics too. He must not be altogether utilitarian.’

“ He was a great man and a wonderful one, but you see he saw ‘ the use of a poet.’ ”

The Socialist is a very fortunate person. He has many gifts, but I think perhaps his choicest possession is a charming little habit of saying pretty things.

“ A fascinating young humbug,” I heard some one who is very fond of him say not long ago. “ He has the trick of saying things just as it is most delightful to hear them.”

But I, who have been quite intimate with him since his birth, have a theory that he is not really

14

a humbug at all, but that he has the luck to think pleasant things, and the power to say frankly and prettily what he thinks. And what luck that is!

He put his arm around my waist and looked up at me with his most dimpled smilingness.

" Yes, Chérie," he said, "thank you for explaining it to me. I understand what you mean. I think I see the use of a poet. And I know what a poet is. You are a poet."

I considered this quite a triumph of lovable courtliness even for him.

" I should like to be," I answered, "even if I couldn't write poetry."

" So should I," he said, "though I am only a boy. I can try to be."

" We will both try," I said.

THE BOY WHO BECAME A SOCIALIST

THE BOY WHO BECAME A SOCIALIST

THE room in which I work in my house in London is called the Japanese room. It is called so because all the furniture and decorations are Japanese. But there are two very un-Japanese decorations. They are the portraits of two boys, who watch me all the time. One, who is about fourteen, stands with his hands in his coat pockets as if he were perhaps looking at a cricket match or a base-ball game; the other is about twelve, and is leaning against an old carved oak cabinet. This last one is the Socialist. You would never imagine it when you looked at his picture. He has such a round, laughing face, and he wears a quaint costume with a long pointed vest, lace ruffles, and paste knee and shoe buckles, and a velvet coat—not at all what you would expect of a person with Socialistic views, and, in fact, it is not the Socialist's usual costume. It was one he wore when he sang a quaint song at a charity concert, and it was so becoming to his plump young body that I wanted a picture of him in it. And yet, notwithstanding his round, dimpled, boy face, and his velvet coat, and lace ruffles, and his brilliant paste buckles, it is he who is the Socialist.

It was in London at the beginning of the last season that I found this out. I had not been aware of it myself before. He came into my room one morning, and the moment he entered I knew that he was filled to the brim with some new exciting idea which he must talk about. I always know when he is in that condition because his face looks rounder and rosier than ever, and such a lot of queer little dimples dance about his mouth.

"Dearest," he said, "I am a Socialist. I just wanted to tell you I am a Socialist," and he thrust his hands into the very bottom of the pockets of his little red and black blazer and sat down firmly on the nearest chair.

It was perhaps a little sudden, but then I am never surprised at anything the Socialist does. I have known him long enough to be quite accustomed to the cheerful activity of his mind. So I only smiled and looked interested—as I felt.

"Are you, dear?" I answered. "When did it begin?"

"Well, you see," he explained, delight and eagerness making quite an illumination of him, "I have been reading the most *beautiful* book. It is the most beautiful book I ever read in all my life. It is by Edward Bellamy, and it is called

'Looking Backward.' I have not quite finished it, and the only thing is, I am so afraid it will turn out at the end to be only a dream. I want it to seem as if it were quite true."

This interested me. I had read the book my-, self, and I thought I should very much like to hear how it had impressed a sturdy twelve-year-old Socialist with his hands in the pockets of a tennis jacket.

It is always interesting to know what boys and girls think of great problems—if they think naturally and through simple spontaneous interest. They have all of life before them; they have the courage and hope that can believe and plan things, and they have the years in which to do the best things to develop plans. It was quite exciting to look at the Socialist, with his glowing face and his strong little clenched boy's hands.

"And the book made you a Socialist?" I said. "What sort of a Socialist?"

He was so full of his subject that he could not sit still. He is never a very still boy. He jumped up and began to walk up and down the room, talking as he walked, and making the most animated gestures.

"The sort that could help to make the kind of world there is in that book," he said. "It made me so excited to read it. Why, if it were true, there would be no more wrong or injustice, or poverty or suffering — there would be no more beggars, or tyrants or idle people—just think of that! And every man would have his own work to do, and he would do it. Oh, why can't it be true? I can't bear it to be only a dream."

One of the charms of the Socialist is that he is so tremendously in earnest about everything. He rides his bicycle, plays cricket or tennis or football, rows and dances, or shouts over a base-ball game, all with equal ardor. He is a boy with an athletic appetite, and a strong, young, growing body — that is the thing that adds to one's interest in his strong, young, growing heart and mind.

"It would be a beautiful dream, in which all sorrow and wrong could be put an end to for ever, wouldn't it?" I said.

He wheeled about and made an animated gesture with his clenched hand.

"But it ought not to be only a dream," he said. "It ought to be real."

"Well," I answered, "of course all great changes and improvements take time, and perhaps even if the ends were accomplished, it would not be exactly in the 'Looking Backward' way—but it wouldn't matter how it was done. And I should think the best beginning would be that all the people who read the book—boys especially, because they have all their years before them —

should make up their minds each to do his part of trying to make it real."

That delighted him. He looked more aglow than ever, and all his dear little dimples showed themselves at once.

" That would do it," he exclaimed, walking up and down with new excitement. " And wouldn't I like to try! It would take years and years, I dare say—it might not come till after my life was over—but oh! if I could be just one of those who *helped* to make it not a dream."

" Then my life would have been worth living," I said, " because I should have been the mother of one of those who helped to make it not a dream. Sit down and let us talk it over."

Then he sat down and we talked it over, and it was delightful. It would have been very interesting to have taken down the Socialist's remarks just as he made them in his vigorous, unadorned, boy English. He wanted all the imperfect laws repealed, all the rich people to be generous, all the poor ones to be given work and good pay, all the weak ones to be taken care of and helped to become strong, everything that was unjust to be righted, all that was bad to be changed into good.

" Only *how* are we to do it ?" he said. " Such a lot of things would have to be changed, wouldn't they ?"

" Well," I said, " you see all the great changes for the better are always made because a number of people make up their minds singly, one by one, you know—that they ought to be brought about. It isn't a hundred thousand people who do a thing all at once in a mass—in the first place a hundred thousand individual minds have to work for themselves singly. You know a lot of boys—how would it do to have a Looking Forward Club, and let every boy be determined to be the fairest, most straightforward, manly, reasonable fellow he can, not only to the club and himself, but to anyone he has to deal with? That would be a beginning."

" So it would," agreed the Socialist.

" Boys have so much to give each other," I said, " if they only thought of it. You know I have had two boys, so I know how interesting their lives are. They are finding out things and having new experiences every day if they have quick minds. For instance, there is your friend Sam, whom I have such a respect for. He has always had to take care of himself. He has sold newspapers and blacked boots all his little boy years in the streets of a big city. Sam is all right, you know. He has a good heart and kind feelings, and it did them no harm that he was ragged and bare-footed, and even sometimes hungry, and think how much he must have learned about business, and self-dependence, and how much he must have seen to touch his heart, and fill him with pity and the wish to be able to help and make things better. Sam is the beginning of an energetic man with his mind all alive. And you are the beginning of another, I hope, and you have lived in an entirely different way, and so each one of you must have so much to tell the other. Sam has watched base-ball games, I have no doubt; you have seen great cricket matches at Lord's. Sam has taken long tramps from one city to another to sell his papers; you have crossed the Atlantic in a big steamer year after year, and have been on familiar terms with sailors and engineers. Sam has sold papers at inaugurations; you have watched the kings and queens, and princes and princesses, and all the grand pageant of the Jubilee. Sam knows how to manage a boot-black business and understands the language of the boys who take care of themselves; you can speak French and understand Italian. Sam knows about ' conventions;' you know about the carnival in Italy, and have driven with your carriage buried in bouquets in the Flower Corso, and have thrown coriandoli and laughed at the mascherati and danced at the great veglone ball. Sam has talked to keen, clever American politicians; you know about world-renowned English statesmen. Between you two boys it appears to me you have a great part of the world and the most interesting sides of life to discuss and compare notes about. I really think, you know, that any one listening while you talked and told each other things might gain quite a respectable education. And think what one might gain from a number of boys all with different lives and different views."

"Only," said the Socialist, "sometimes a boy can't express himself."

"That is what you would have to think of in the most practical way," I answered. "Some boys chance to have words, and some are, perhaps, not ready with them. If you are a good Socialist, you must remember that gifts are only workman's tools. The boy without words may have something else—some thoughts and views that are worth ever so much more. You must not laugh or treat him lightly if he speaks badly. See if you can't lend him your tools in some way."

The Socialist has words, and he used them in his most delightful manner. We were quite happy together. We disposed of almost all the problems of the day in about an hour, and we did not leave a wrong that was not uprooted.

Darling Socialist, he is so energetic.

"I should like to begin this very day," he said, walking up and down with his fists in the pockets of the red and black blazer.

He might in a small way, I said.

He turned to look at me.

" Are you going to laugh?" he said.

" Far from it," I answered, though I confess I was smiling a little, but then I am always smiling more or less when I talk with the Socialist.

" One always has to begin with the little things, and I was thinking of something that would be a part of the big scheme at all events. You see one of the points is that every one is to do his own work and not léave any of it for the others to do. Now suppose there was a boy—"

The Socialist dimpled and gave a dramatic little tap to the breast of the gay blazer.

" Well," I continued, "suppose he had a habit of leaving things on the chairs and tables—tennis rackets and cricket bats in the hall, books and hats and papers anywhere they dropped. Of course somebody else who had something else to do would have to pick them up and put them away, and of course that would take the time that belonged fairly to their other work—and it would not be fair or Socialistic. You see the point is that if you are a good Socialist you must not leave your work to be done by someone else. Isn't that true?"

" Yes," answered the Socialist, quite beaming over the idea and laughing that dear little laugh which to this day brings back to me the years when he was almost a baby, with a lot of curly bright hair and a face that laughed all the time, and everyone laughed back at. "If you are a good Socialist, you will hang up your hat and not leave your bat in the hall or your racket on the piano."

"That is the principle," I answered, while he hugged me with the red and black sleeves, "though I don't think Mr. Bellamy once mentioned it."

BIRDIE

BIRDIE

SHE was a little girl I knew when first I was married, and I shall always remember her as she was then, when she was seven years old and we were intimate acquaintances. She was in fact at that time the only very intimate acquaintance I had, though I knew a good many people. We were about the same age, though it is true I had lived some time longer than she had. But there was something considerate about Birdie which made me feel that after all they did not make so much difference between us—those few years which had entitled me to be married. She was much more mature and serious in some ways than I was, but that probably arose from her greater experience. She was the mother of a most interesting family, and I had not yet been introduced to Boy and the Socialist.

It was indeed through a member of her family that we became such intimate friends. It was through Miss Anna, who had been stricken with the measles, and through an incompleteness in the matter of rash which was supposed to be "striking in" instead of "coming out," was giving her parent the gravest anxiety.

Miss Anna was *not* a young lady, as might at first be supposed. She was a large doll, and though she looked young, she was quite advanced in years—for a doll—for she was eighteen years old. She had been the doll of Birdie's aunt, she was universally admired and respected, and her head was made of china. The first time I saw her I had driven out to see Birdie's mamma at the charming house in the country where they lived.

I think that as soon as I entered the room I saw Miss Anna, and observed that she was an invalid. She was lying in invalid state upon a sofa, her kid arms were carefully tucked away under the shawl that covered her, and her blue china eyes were fixed rather staringly upon space. Evidently she was concentrating all the energies of a gigantic china intellect upon her illness whatever it might be (I have since thought that—probably fearing its effect on her complexion, which was extremely red and white—she herself had determined that the rash should not "come out").

Having a strong private affection for dolls — (I find it even increases with years. I cannot to-day pass the windows of Le Petit Nain Bleu, in the Boulevard des Capucines, without loitering) —I could not help casting an occasional interested glance at the sofa while I talked to Birdie's mamma—and the Major ("The Major" was Birdie's papa).

But suddenly my interest was greatly increased. The door opened, and a slender delicate little girl came in, and seeming to think that as the grown-up people were talking she would be unnoticed, went with the most serious and absorbed little face to the sofa. She was a *very* pretty child. I think that I can best explain what she expressed to me by using a French word, and saying that she looked *spirituelle*. She was very slight, and moved very softly, she had fine brown hair, which hung loose, a pure fair skin, with a faint rose-leaf color, and a delicate small face, with the clearest innocent golden-brown eyes I ever saw.

All the unusualness and charm of the small face one could not see in the first moment. One would always see a pretty, refined child, but it was only after I knew her well that I explained to myself what her unique charm was.

The clear eyes had the beauty of a crystal pool in the deep forest, a pool which had never been disturbed, and had never reflected anything less sweet in nature than sunlight filtered through the trees, and friendly little birds chirping as they came to drink and bathe their wings. They were such happy eyes, such believing eyes, such childish, dreaming eyes—one loved them as soon as she lifted the long curled lashes.

She was busying herself so anxiously about the sofa that I glanced questioningly at the Major.

"Oh, that is Birdie," he said, with a kindly and slightly humorous smile. "Birdie, come and shake hands with Mrs. Burnett."

Birdie crossed the room and gave me her hand and a sweet little smile.

I kept the hand in mine and gave her a smile in return, but I tried to make it sympathetic, because I recognized at once that the case of the invalid on the sofa was not one to trifle with. I saw it in Birdie's countenance.

"I am very glad to see you," I said; "your papa was talking to me about you. But I am sorry you have illness in your family. I hope it is not very serious."

I was not laughing at all—I would not have laughed for worlds in that serious little face. I tried quickly to imagine that I was seven, and that I was right in the midst of a belief that my favorite china child was ill, and I knew it would disturb my feelings very much if I were suddenly called from her bedside to shake hands with a bride who made light of me.

And in one second I saw in Birdie's clear gold-brown eyes a look of relief and appreciation.

She made friends with me on the spot without any further preliminaries.

"I am afraid it *is* serious," said she, looking back at the sofa. "Miss Anna has the measles very badly, and you know sometimes the measles turn out dreadfully serious."

"Yes," I said, "the danger is, you know, if they take the least cold. If you can just get them through without taking cold they are all right; but if they catch cold, and it strikes in, it's the most anxious thing. Would it disturb her if I went and looked at her?"

"I should be very glad if you would look at her," said Birdie.

I saw her mamma and the Major glance at each other as we left them, and the Major's humorous eyes looked in a very quiet way more humorous than ever, but he did not laugh at all. I discovered afterwards that he never disturbed Birdie's beliefs and fancies, or treated them with any disrespect which would spoil them for her.

"You see she is flushed," I said, having looked at Miss Anna. "If you keep her warm, and give her hot things to drink, I dare say she will have quite a beautiful rash before night. I had a wax one once who had scarlatina, and I think I saved her life with hot camomile tea."

When I went away Birdie and I were no longer acquaintances, but friends, and our friendship was destined to be a very interesting one.

At first Birdie lived in the country, and I in the town a few miles away, and during the hot Southern summer my visits to her home used to be a great relief to me. The air was so much cooler and fresher there, and there were so many tall trees and so much shade. Her house was built in the midst of a beautiful grove of pine and oak trees, and it was chiefly while wandering under their shadows that we had our most interesting conversations. It was there I found out one of Birdie's prettiest fancies, which ended in our spending together one of the most delightful mornings of my life. It was a lovely summer morning, and we were rambling about together, gathering a flower or so as we talked, or stopping to catch a bird, or bending down to examine some interesting little insect in the grass. I had indeed gathered a good deal of information on various subjects, because " The Major," who had been a Confederate officer, had become a Professor in a well-known Southern university, and he and his little daughter, who were great friends, were in the habit of exploring the woods in a happy sort of way together, so Birdie really knew many things about birds and insects and rocks and flowers.

She had been saying something to me about a

certain kind of tall swaying grass I admired, and she quietly stooped, tied the long blades together, and bent them carefully down in the part where the knot was.

"What are you doing that for?" I asked.

"Ah!" she answered quite simply, lifting her clear eyes with a smile, "it is for the fairies."

"For the fairies?" I said.

"Well, you see," she said, glancing round at the wind - swept, sun - dappled field flowers and grasses, "there are so many of them here. They live in the country, you know; they don't like the town to live in — they only go there to see people they are fond of. Riverside" (that was the name of their country house) "is full of them, and they are so fond of swinging. So when I come out I tie the tops of the long grasses and bend them over. It makes a little swing, you see."

I saw that it did, and I saw, too, that she had not a shadow of a doubt that it would sway to and fro with the light weight of a fairy before it had time to wither.

"I do a great many things for them," she said. "And they are so glad, and they do so like me."

"Let us make some more swings," I said, kneeling down and beginning to look for the tallest grasses. "And tell me what other things you do. Do you know them—the fairies I mean?"

"Oh, I know them," she answered, busying herself with another swing, " but I have never seen them. I just do things to make them happy. You see they are so tiny, tiny, tiny, that it isn't easy to see them. They think we are giants, and they are rather frightened of us until they know we are their friends, and they run away and hide in flower-cups and under leaves and in the grass. They know now that I won't hurt them, so perhaps I *may* see them some day. I hope I shall. I never do *anything* that might make them afraid of me, and I am always trying to please them."

"I wish I could see them," I said ; " I always did so want to see a fairy."

"They are so pretty !" she said. " They are dressed in clothes made of flowers, or spun out of sparkling spiders' webs, and they have diamonds made of dew-drops, and sometimes their ball-dresses are spun out of sunshine and moonshine and that light white morning mist."

Nothing could have been sweeter or more perfectly simple and natural than her happy sincerity. She spoke of the fairies as if she were speaking of humming birds or butterflies or bees. I felt as if they might be swarming about us at that very minute. I tried to pretend to myself that it was true, and I succeeded pretty well too.

"WHAT ARE YOU DOING THAT FOR?" I ASKED

I always liked fairies, and it was delightful to kneel there in the warm scented long grass and talk and act as if they were real.

" Have they balls and ball-dresses ? " I asked. " But of course they have, because I've read about them."

" They are *very* fond of balls," she answered. " They dance every night there is moonlight. They have asked Miss Anna to their balls—they are not afraid of her. They think she is a sort of relation."

" Did she ever go ? " I inquired.

" Well, no ! She's small compared with us, you know, but she is big compared to fairies, and I think she was afraid she might tread on some of them, and that would have spoiled all their party."

" So it would," I replied. " But it would have been nice if she could have gone and sat down carefully, and just looked on. Then she could have told you about it. Now we have made swings enough ; what could we do next ? "

" I have just thought of something very important," said Birdie. " There is a full moon to-night, and they are going to have a *grand* ball in the grove before the house, and I was going to prepare their ball-room under the oak tree that has a hollow in it. They use the hollow for a bed-room to take off their things in, and if any of them bring babies they want very soft moss beds to lay them on."

"Do they bring their children sometimes?" I asked.

"They do just now. Roseleaf and Blossom both have babies, and fairy babies are *so* tiny they daren't leave them alone, because the least breath of wind might blow them away."

We left the fairy swings and went to the oak at once, and began to work in the most earnest manner.

First we cleared away all twigs and fallen leaves and bits of pebble from under the tree, and made a charming smooth place to dance on. Then we made a fine moss carpet and bordered it with fresh leaves, and, as a finishing touch, we made moss seats to rest on between the dances. The supper - room required much more work. First we had to find a piece of " diamond stone," as Birdie called it, which was the right shape and size, and white enough and sparkling enough to make a table. She said the sparkles were really diamonds, and the fairies did not like chairs or tables without diamonds. The plates and dishes were made of small curled rose petals, and the cups for the fairy wine (which was dew, Birdie told me) were the cups of the tiniest flowers we could find. It was very pretty when it was all finished, and then we prepared the bed-

room in the hollow of the tree. That was car-
peted with leaves and had moss beds and pillows
for Roseleaf's and Blossom's babies. Indeed, it
was all so charming that it made me wish to be
a fairy myself — but that was nothing new, because I had always wished I was a fairy. Birdie
was quite satisfied when we left the tree, and on
our way back to the house we talked in the most
animated way of what the fairies would say when
they saw our preparations for them, and what
they would do, and how much they would like
us for being so friendly.

It was a charming morning, which I shall never
forget. I had many charming mornings with
Birdie. Our friendship grew more and more
intimate, and at the end of the summer her
family left their house in the country and took
a house in town, which was just on the opposite
side of the street from mine.

But before that, I had a delightful visit from
Miss Anna. Birdie and I pretended that she was
obliged to visit some fashionable mineral springs
after her measles. So I carried her to my house
in town and kept her there. I think I wrote one
or two letters from her to her mother describing
her gay life at Montvale or White Sulphur. But
the truth was that Miss Anna was really with me,
and I was making her some new things to wear.
I remember there were some pocket handker-

chiefs among them, and when she went back to Riverside she was newly dressed, and her mother found her looking very well and much improved by the mineral waters.

It was after her family had taken possession of the town house that I nearly made a fatal error in speaking of Miss Anna to her mother.

Birdie was sitting in a swing in the garden and I was on a low seat near her, and in speaking of Miss Anna's many accomplishments, I said, " She is the nicest doll I ever knew."

The most startled expression came into her sensitive little face, and she put up her hand as if to stop me.

" Oh, *don't*, Mrs. Burnett!" she exclaimed. " Oh, please, hush! Never say she is a *doll*. I never mention the word before her. It would hurt her feelings so!"

" Would it really?" I said. " I'm so sorry I said it. She didn't hear it, though. She is in her room asleep."

" Miss Anna doesn't *know* she is a doll," said Birdie. " She never dreams it. She thinks she is just like us, and I could not bear to have her find out that her head is made of china—or that it seems like that to people who don't love her. It isn't china to me — and neither are her arms kid—but then I'm her mother."

Never again was I guilty of inferring that Miss

Anna was a doll—never so long as I knew her. I should not mention it now only I know she never reads papers, and my dear little Birdie, who must be a grown - up young lady by this time, would understand how far I am from meaning any disrespect to her dear old china memory.

It interested me very much to read afterwards in one of Miss Phelps's books, of a little girl who expressed exactly Birdie's idea, and I wondered if perhaps Miss Phelps had not heard of it from a real child as I did.

It was very absorbing when Boy was introduced to Birdie and Miss Anna and myself. Birdie's experience as a parent was very useful to me in my first venture, and she had a very good opinion of Boy, though I think we were both quite frank in admitting that just at first he was more big than exactly beautiful. I went abroad the next spring, and when I kissed Birdie for the last time I thought we should be intimate friends again in about two years. I wrote a story for her while I was away. She and her brothers and sisters published a little paper in their own house and she asked me to write them something. I sent it to her from London. It was called " Behind the White Brick," and has since been published with other short stories in a book. But since those days chance has placed us almost at different ends of the earth.

Birdie must be by now a grown-up young lady. Remembering her delicate *spirituelle* little face and translucent golden - brown eyes, I feel sure she is fair to look upon ; remembering her pretty innocent fancies and tender beliefs, I am sure she must be lovable and sweet. When I think of her, as I often do, knowing how many fairy things seem to fade away as one grows from a child to a woman, I cannot help saying to myself wistfully, " I hope she still believes in the fairies, and I hope—because she is so gentle and tender—she sometimes sees one."

THE TINKER'S TOM

THE TINKER'S TOM

I SAW him only twice and had only short conversations with him, but without intending or knowing it he gave me ideas of a strange life of which before I knew nothing, and which, nevertheless, hundreds—even thousands perhaps—live.

There are single individuals who live a life something like it in America, but they are called tramps, and certainly do not seem to be usually people with large families which they carry with them accompanied by pots and kettles and numberless children, which give a curious air of domesticity to their ramblings.

But in England they are a distinct class. When you pass on a country road a rickety covered cart, loaded with shabby, dilapidated odds and ends, drawn by a small donkey led by a dilapidated man or woman and accompanied by a drove of children, you say at once, " Ah, there are some travelling tinkers ! " And you generally add, " And what a lot of babies."

And when you come during your walk through country lanes to a wearily grazing donkey or a

very thin, rough horse, hobbled with a piece of
rope and cropping the grass by the hedges, then
you say, " Some tinkers have stopped near here."
And before many minutes you are likely to find a
queer encampment, boiling its battered kettle and
spreading its poor belongings on the roadside
grass quite near you.

There is generally the cart as a sort of back-
ground. It has been emptied and its awning has
been taken off to make a sort of arched tent. It
never seemed possible to me that there could be
room for more of the tinkers than the tinker
mother and the youngest tinker baby to sleep
under it, but it seemed possible to get so many
things into the cart itself when it was loaded,
that one could not feel it safe to limit the capacity of the awning. Ragged pieces of bed cloth-
ing and tattered bits of garments hang on the
bushes of gorse and bramble ; there are battered
cooking utensils, and if the Tinker has jobs in
hand there is fire and he probably sits hammer-
ing by it.

The truth is, you know, that there is only one
Tinker in the family, and he is the head of it—the
owner of the donkey or horse, the cart, the awning, the worn looking woman with the babies, the
children of all sizes and ages, the hungry dog, in
fact the whole paraphernalia.

But still we always spoke of the whole family

as "tinkers," and it seemed quite natural to say, "The tinker mother was gathering mushrooms with five of the little tinkers," or "I'm afraid the tinker baby has got the whooping - cough," or "Did you notice what a nice face the tinker donkey has?"

Every one who knows England, knows the beautiful country roads and lanes, with the unending hawthorn hedges and the grass-covered banks they grow on, where a footsore traveller can often find such a convenient resting-place. It is under the hedges the little tinkers are born, I think; under the hedges they grow up, under the hedges they dream their childish dreams and think their young thoughts—but somehow I cannot help hoping that it is not under the hedges that many of them die—though after all I could imagine a little tinker falling asleep softly for the last time, if the time were a warm spring morning, and the hawthorn were in bloom, and the English sky was blue and dappled with fleecy little white clouds above.

It was under the hedges we made the acquaintance of the Tinker's Tom. We mean my dearest friend and I, who during that happy year and the next were always together.

We had been in London during the Jubilee season, and at the end of it, as I was not well, my doctor had ordered me away to the Norfolk or

Suffolk coast, where it seemed I should find the bracing air I needed.

Popular and populous English watering places are not interesting or soothing, so after several unsatisfactory pilgrimages we found at last a dear belated little fishing village in Suffolk, where there was one street of quaint houses, a wonderful little hotel on a cliff, which had been transformed from a gentleman's shooting box into a pretty resting place for summer loiterers, a few small bay-windowed houses with " Apartments to let " in the most prominent panes, a few little shops, and a circulating library where one could buy toys and china drinking mugs inscribed in gold letters with " A present from Southwold." One could also get from there odd volumes of Mrs. Braddon, and works by the author of " The Heir of Redclyffe," three volumes at a time for a sixpence a week, and the name of the proprietress was, I think, Miss Chicksby.

But even Southwold did not seem quite secluded enough for me, so after a week at the wonderful little hotel which seemed so modern and æsthetic in the midst of its quaint surroundings, we found a place even more primitive—an old farm house in a green lane a few miles away —a veritable English farm house with white walls and a red roof, diamond-paned windows, thatched farm buildings, and rambling farm yards.

It would be very easy to write pages about Elm Farm and what we did there, of the delights of the boys who made hay and reaped and gleaned, who vowed eternal friendship with the cow men and harvesters, who spent rapturous hours tend-ing sheep with the little shepherd, while he sang ancient Suffolk ballads about squires who loved milkmaids, and ploughmen who loved ladies; who became gloriously intimate with the small "pig-minder" and his family, who went "rabbit-ing" with the farmer, and were so blissfully happy that when in the autumn we left Suffolk to go to Italy, they began their journey in silence, leaning back in their corners of the carriage, their arms folded, and tears in their eyes.

But this sketch is to be about the little tinker, and the boys did not know him.

In a place such as the one I describe, there are only two things one can do when one is not writ-ing letters or reading the odd volumes from the circulating library. One is to drive, and the other is to walk through the green lanes, over the country roads, and through the tiny villages with their queer irregular streets and quaint cottages in which the small windows are so bright, their bits of white curtain so clean, and the geraniums and fuchsias and lobelias in the pots adorning them, so marvellously flourishing. So we drove and walked a great deal, and though we did not limit ourselves, and rambled over the country generally as mere explorers, we had naturally one or two favorite walks which we took again and again.

The one we liked best took us past woods and along a green banked and hedged country road until we reached a branching lane which led us to the thickly grassed top of the line of cliffs by the sea. A resting place seemed to have been prepared there. At the highest point of the cliffs where one could look far down on the prettiest curve of shore, and could see the widest stretch of white sand and sea, and the idlest floating gulls, and boats with white or brown sails, there was a little hollow curve in the grassy earth which seemed to fit one's body like a cradle. One could lie idly there and watch the gulls and the sky, and look down over the edge at the scattered flames of scarlet, which were clumps of vagabond poppies, that in some spirit of adventure had left their corn-fields and scrambled and clung to the cliffs' side.

We were going there one morning, and were walking along the country road, when we saw a cavalcade slowly approaching us.

It was not an imposing cavalcade, but it interested us. First there was a very small and shaky cart. It was loaded with things to sleep on and wear and cook in, until one wondered how it could possibly be drawn along without falling over to one side or the other. The things seemed principally bundles of rags and shabbiness, and the donkey who drew it was very small, and had a patient ragged dilapidated air herself. But she was pulling her burden along unrebelliously, and keeping her eye on the baby donkey which trotted by her side.

Of course we knew she was a tinker's donkey and was pulling a tinker's belongings, as she had probably been pulling them all through the summer through various counties. The tinker himself was strolling by the cart with a short pipe in his mouth, and on the other side was the tinker's wife pushing the remnants of a perambulator with two babies in it and several dingy bundles.

But the chief feature of the procession was, to my mind, the person who was holding the donkey by a piece of rope, and boldly leading it along by the head.

This person might have been four years old, and must have been the third baby of the tinker, and one would have imagined he was young enough to have been in the perambulator if there had been room for him.

But he plainly preferred leading the procession and the donkey, and was not a little proud of his position.

I wish that I could say he was pretty, but I cannot. He was neither beautiful nor picturesque, but I could see he had a bold and adventurous spirit, and I liked him for it.

He had a plain sunburnt little face, and tangled light sunburnt hair which stuck through the rim and crown of the most dilapidated straw hat. He was dressed in a dingy and ragged frock which had evidently descended to him from some of the other little tinkers and which flopped about his legs curiously, but he seemed to be on good terms with the donkey, and the donkey did not seem to feel his guidance detrimental to her dignity.

The remainder of the procession consisted of the rest of the little tinkers—an endless number of various ages and sizes it seemed to me; scattered at irregular distances along the road behind the cart, until the last ones seemed, as it were, to melt into the distance.

" I wonder where they will stop to-night," I said to my friend; " and where they stopped last, and how many of them can get under the awning." The very next day we found out where they stopped.

We were going to our cliff again, and as we turned the corner by the coppice into the road we saw a light blue smoke curling up out of a sort of dip or hollow by the roadside.

"Oh," we exclaimed, "there are our tinkers!" And there they were. The cart was unloaded and the contents spread over the grass and bushes. And one realized what a wonderful capacity for holding things it must have had. All the hollow was occupied. The awning had been made into the usual tent of refuge, under it the babies were sleeping, their mother was seated on the ground near them putting some stitches into a ragged coat, the tinker's fire was lighted and beside it the Tinker himself was sitting mending some old pot or pan or kettle.

Except the babies there were no other little tinkers to be seen. It was a beautiful morning, and there are probably plenty of amusing things for little tinkers to do in fine weather in the country.

"Perhaps," my friend and I said to each other as we walked along, "there are times when it is not so unpleasant to be a tinker and have one's household goods drawn all over England by a donkey, and live under the hedges."

We walked on some distance, talking this over and inventing plans by which such a life might be made comfortable as well as interesting, and we were just in the midst of building a tinker's cart with all the conveniences of a Mayfair bedroom when we saw on the roadside grass two donkeys grazing, one lying down, the other standing up, and at a little distance a small boy sitting under the hedge guarding them.

"The tinker's donkeys," we said, "and one of the tinker boys."

The baby donkey attracted us and we went to talk to it, and found its mother equally interesting notwithstanding her worn gray coat and her shabby ears. We decided that it was her expression we liked and which was her chief charm. She had such a gentle, unworldly face as if even years of pulling the tinker's cart had not made her lose her faithful patience with things. I wondered if she felt at all depressed by the thought that her pretty, fluffy, gray baby might be a tinker's donkey too.

We patted and stroked them both, and as we were bending over the mother, who was lying down, the tinker boy called out in a friendly voice, "Get up now, Jinny. Stand on yer feet an' let the ladies see yer."

That was enough to begin any country-road acquaintance with, and we at once included the little tinker in our conversation with the donkeys and presently edged over to him.

He was a nice little fellow about ten years old and had seemingly monopolized the good looks of the family. He had a well-featured face and light hair that curled a little, and a pair of big, candid, blue eyes—really quite beautiful blue eyes. He was like his donkey in one respect, namely that he had an expression which was attractive.

He was sitting on the bank under the hedge, and his coarse ragged little shirt was open at the breast, and he plainly had something hidden inside it, for we could see an active wriggling going on.

"What have you got there?" we asked.

He laughed and put his hand into his shirt bosom. "Now, Spotty," he said, "come out o' there. What are yer 'idin' fer?"

And he pulled out and exhibited quite proudly a pretty little fox terrier puppy.

Both my friend and I are fond of dogs, and of course we began to exclaim and admire, and took the little fellow in our arms, where he wriggled and kissed us in his puppy fashion, using his active red tongue as affectionately as if we had been quite old acquaintances. He was too young a puppy to discriminate.

"He's a good un," said the little tinker. "He's a real good un. His mother was one o' Lord Dunham's. One of 'is gamekeepers give 'im me. We stopped on a 'eath near the park an' the gamekeeper was a wonderful nice man." ("Wonderful" seemed to be a much used adjective in Suffolk. Our little maid at the farm told us among other things that the rector of the parish was "a wonderful cross gentleman.")

"He's very pretty," I said. "I didn't see him yesterday. But I didn't see you either when we passed the cart on the road. It was your cart, wasn't it? I thought I knew the donkeys again."

"Yes, my lady," nodding his head towards the part of the road where we had passed the encampment. "We're stoppin' in the dip there."

"It seems a good place," I said. "It looked quite .comfortable when we came by it just now."

"It's all right when it's fine," he answered; "but it rained wonderful 'ard last night, an' it swum us all out. It come streamin' down an' floodin' everythin' an' we 'ad all of us to get up."

"How many of you are there?"

"'Leven of us with father an' mother—nine of us children. There's one of the little uns playin' down the road there; that's Johnny."

Under the hedge in the distance we could see a dilapidated hat and flopping frock, which seemed to be finding amusement somehow, and which I recognized at once as being worn by the infant we had met leading the donkey and cart.

"Isn't he rather little to be so far off by himself?" I inquired.

"Johnny? Oh, no, my lady! Johnny's four years old, an' he knows 'ow to take care of 'isself. He never wants no one to bother 'im. He just comes along by 'isself. He likes the donkeys an' they likes 'im. He brings 'em grass an' thistles

HE PULLED OUT AND EXHIBITED QUITE PROUDLY A PRETTY LITTLE FOX TERRIER PUPPY

an' things to eat, an' when he's tired he just drops down by Jinny an' falls asleep ag'inst her."

It was exactly what my estimate of Johnny, as he had walked floppingly but sturdily by the donkey the day before, would have led me to suppose, that he " wouldn't want no one to bother 'im."

" And you just travel about with the cart all the time," I said, wishing artfully to encourage conversation.

" All the summer time," answered the small tinker. " In the winter we goes into the Union."

The Union is the poorhouse, but he spoke quite cheerfully and simply, as if this life, which spent its summers by the roadside and its winters in the poorhouse, were the most natural one in the world.

I felt a delicacy about asking questions, but I wanted to ask so many. I wanted to know how eleven people were distributed in the Union, and if they continued to be tinkers, if donkeys were taken in, and if not, where they were kept, and how Johnny managed to amuse himself without them.

" What is your name? " I asked, wishing that this commonplace query might lead to further intimacy, and wondering if it would.

" Tom," he answered. And that set me to wondering if tinkers had no surnames. It did not

17

seem to occur to him that " Tom " was not enough for any little tinker.

Suddenly he looked up at me with a questioning in his blue eyes.

" Would you like this 'ere little dog, my lady?" he asked.

" I am afraid I could not take care of him," I replied. " I am going away and shall be travelling about all the time, and he's very young, you know. Do you want to sell him ? "

" I'd give 'im away," he said. " He's 'ungry. I can't give 'im enough to eat. He ain't 'ad no breakfast, nor yet no supper."

" Poor little dog," I said. " Had he nothing at all ? "

" I 'adn't nothin' myself," said the little tinker, quite uncomplainingly, almost cheerfully. " We 'adn't neither of us no supper nor no breakfast. If I'd 'ad any I'd a give 'im some. An' 'e's little, you know, my lady; 'e ain't nothin' but a pup, an' he don't understand."

The inference seemed to be that being a little tinker he *did* understand himself that it was altogether to be expected that there were numerous occasions when one had to go without breakfast and supper, and that regular meals were merely the sumptuous eccentricities of the " gentry." And he was such a nice little tinker, with his good-looking face and his blue eyes !

Being an improvident, indiscriminate sort of person, I am not always allowed to carry my purse when I go out, but this morning I did manage to find half a crown, which I handed over as quickly as possible to the tinker's Tom and the fox-terrier puppy.

" That will buy you both some breakfast, won't it ? " I said.

" 'Arf a crown ! " pulling his forelock delightedly. " Thank ye, my lady. Yes, my lady, it'll keep us quite a good bit, Spotty an' me."

Possibly Spotty suspected something friendly and agreeable in the conversation. He wriggled delightedly and rolled over on the grass, wagging his short tail with such an air of affectionate rapture that both my friend and I felt it necessary to kneel down by his side on the turf and pat him and help him to more active rollings.

The tinker's Tom looked on with such a brightly beaming face that I could not help feeling that there must be something more for him to do in the world than merely sit under the hedges in the day, be " swum out " at night, and "go into the Union " in the winter.

" Do you ever stay anywhere long enough to be able to get any work to do for the farmers?" I asked. " There are two or three boys who do things for our farmer at Reydon, where we are staying."

The tinker's Tom looked at me with a smile in his frank blue eyes. I suppose he thought, in an amiable way, that such simpleness was just like "the gentry" who had only roadside acquaintance with tinkers.

"They don't want such as us, my lady," he answered. "The farmers don't like the likes of us."

He did not say it at all sadly. He was quite cheerful and resigned about it. His blue eyes had no cloud in them.

"But why not?" I asked. "The shepherd boy at Reydon is no bigger than you."

"'Tain't the bigness, my lady," he said. "I could watch sheep well enough. There was a farmer in Devonshire took me in to mind sheep once, but some one made trouble for me, and he believed 'em. They allus believe things about such as us. They said I beat the sheep. What would I want to beat a sheep for?" with a reasoning air.

Really I could not imagine what anyone—even the most ferocious little tinker—could wish to beat a sheep for. Among my acquaintances at Reydon I numbered a whole flock of sheep with whom I was on calling terms. I mean, that my friend and I used to call upon them by going to their meadow, and standing outside the barred gate, uttering all sorts of queer little sounds in the hope of hitting upon the one which would attract their attention. We tried all sorts of little noises—such as one calls horses, and dogs, and cows, and chickens, and pigs with, and we used to laugh a great deal at the perfectly apparent ineffectualness of them. But we always managed to attract the sheep's attention and bring them huddling together in a woolly mass around the gate, where they stood and stared at us with their unmeaning, clear, amber eyes, and silly, gentle faces uplifted. We used to wonder if we did not look as silly to them as they did to us, but we both agreed it would be very difficult to decide what a sheep was thinking about, or if it was thinking at all.

Remembering that flock of gentle, silly faces, I could not possibly answer Tom's query as to why he should wish to beat a sheep.

"I am sure you did not beat them," I said.

"But all the same I lost my place," he answered. Then he gave me a very friendly look indeed.

"Are you coming by 'ere again," he said, "when you come from your walk, my lady?"

"Yes," I answered. "Why?"

"Because when I was up the road this mornin', I see a wonderful big mushroom, an' I could go an' get it, an' 'ave it 'ere for you when you come back."

"That would be very kind of you," I said. "But I'll tell you what you shall do at the same time.   If you know where there are mushrooms, you shall go and gather me a basket full, and bring them to Elm Farm, and sell them to me. That will be something for you and Spotty."

He looked so pleased, and pulled his front lock so enthusiastically, that Spotty rolled on the grass, and wagged his tail in wriggling ecstasy.   I am sure he understood.

We left them talking to each other under the hedge, the two donkeys browsing a few feet away. When we returned they were gone, and when we passed the hollow near the wood the tinker was eating some bread and cheese, and Johnny was examining the mended kettle, probably with a view to a possible entry into the tinkering profession.

The next morning Tom brought the mushrooms.   They were very nice, and I paid him well for them.

" Would you like some water cresses, my lady ?" he asked.

" Yes," I answered.   "And as I have not the proper change, you can keep the extra shilling to pay for them.",

I had a very clever demure little English maid at that time.   She was a Londoner, and I always felt she thought me very unsophisticated in my dealings with what she called the " lower classes." She never expressed this by any disrespectful look, for she was the most well-bred young person. But she had a subdued little smile in her eye sometimes. She had come to the door to take the mushrooms, and when the tinker's Tom turned away, I saw her look down sedately.

"What is it, Millington?" I asked.

Her respectful demure little smile deepened.

"He won't come back, ma'am," she said.

"But why not?" I inquired.

If she had not been so very well-bred a young person, I feel sure she would have giggled.

"Because he has got the shilling, ma'am," she answered. "If you wanted the cresses you should have kept the shilling till he brought them, ma'am."

"Oh, Millington," I said, "he has such a nice little face—and he brought the mushrooms."

"Yes, 'm—but he wasn't paid for the mushrooms in advance. I know the ways of those people, ma'am."

I thought of what Tom had said of people's not "liking the likes of us," and I felt rather uncomfortable.

"Well, we must wait and see," I said; "but I cannot help believing in his nice blue eyes. And I didn't care about the cresses really, but I wanted to give him the shilling, and let him feel he had earned it. But I hope he will bring them—poor little tinker."

He did not bring them. Two or three days later we left Suffolk to begin our journey to Italy, and we had not seen the tinker's Tom again. When we spoke of him, Millington's quiet, pretty, little face wore a demure, repressed smile. It is quite true that she knew more about tinkers as a class than my friend and I did. And yet, to this day, I have always preferred to think that, perhaps, there was a *reason* why the cresses were not brought—perhaps they were hard to find, and Tom did not realize that we were going away so soon,—perhaps one of the donkeys was ill, or strayed away, and he had to attend to it,—perhaps Johnny had strayed away himself in search of adventure, and had to be found,—perhaps somebody had caught cold the night it rained so " wonderful 'ard," and they were "swum out,"—it might be one of the babies—or both—got the croup. There might be so many reasons why a little tinker could not keep an appointment. And when one does not know positively, it is so much pleasanter to believe a good thing than a bad one. It may not be as sharp, but I am sure it is better, and makes one happier, and perhaps better oneself, and less capable of evil. At any rate, if one thinks a few minutes one can find a dozen possible good reasons, which might balance against that single bad one, which Millington was respectfully convinced was the right one—namely, that having

the shilling in advance, he did not feel it necessary to produce the water cresses.   And so when
I think of the tinker's Tom, I always tell myself it
must have been any one of the dozen but that.

THE QUITE TRUE STORY OF
AN OLD HAWTHORN TREE

THE QUITE TRUE STORY OF AN OLD HAWTHORN TREE

WHEN it was young it was very happy. It stood in the deep grass where daisies and buttercups grew, and sleepy, kind-eyed cows used to lie under its shade, and birds used to build their nests in its branches, and bring up their families and cuddle together, twittering when it rained, and chirping and singing on the twigs when the sun came out and made the air sweet with a warm, fresh earthy odor, and changed the raindrops into jewels of all colors.

It was a tree with an affectionate nature, and it was very fond of the birds, and always rustled a praise of their singing, and tried to hold its leaves close together to make a shelter for them when it rained. It was so kind to everything that chirped in its branches or rested under them, that it was a great favorite. There was always the greatest haste in the spring, in nest-building time, among the young couples to secure the best places in the Hawthorn Tree, and sometimes quite hasty marriages had been known to take place, so that the bride and groom might be in good time and have the choice of the nooks among the branches.

And how sweet it was when the pink and white buds began to peep out and grow bigger, and pinker, and whiter every day, until, some fine morning, the whole tree was a mass of fragrant blossom, and the air all around it was perfumed. Then the little children used to come to gather "the may," as they called it, and roll about on the grass, and dance and sing, and make wreaths for their heads, and have little feasts in the shade, and enjoy themselves until they were tired, and had to go home and leave the Hawthorn Tree to the birds' twitter and the soft warm night wind again.

When it grew older and sad times came and all was changed, even to the very air it breathed, the Hawthorn Tree used to remember those days with an aching heart.

"Oh," it used to sigh with all its leaves, "if I could only bloom again as I did then, if I could only see the children dancing, and see them with rosy faces and laughing eyes, instead of always so pale and sad and dirty. Everything is dirty now, even the birds have soot on their wings, and can't keep their nests clean."

The change in its happy life had come about so gradually that the Hawthorn Tree could scarcely

tell when first it had begun. It had an idea, however, that the first signs of it appeared on a spring
morning when it had noticed years and years ago
that the smoke of great London town seemed
nearer. It had been very busy blooming at the
time, and it was not quite sure that it was not
mistaken, but later in the year, when it had more
time to notice, it began to be quite certain that
somehow the smoke had advanced more into the
country. This puzzled it very much for a long
time : it did not know how long, but there came
a time when it heard a sort of explanation. It
heard it from two laborers who stopped to sit
down and rest under it on their way home after
their day's work. " Lunnon town," said one of
them, wiping his brow with his rough hand,
" Lunnon town, it do be growin' wonderful."

" So it be, man ; so it be," answered the other.

" A-growin' and a-spreadin' over all the land,"
said the first; " whether it be for good or bad
there's no knowin', but Squire, I hear him swear-
in' t'other day, and sayin' that buildin' was goin'
on so fast that a body could taste smoke when
a' swallowed his tankard o' ale. An' a' said
'twouldn't be no time before the streets would be
all round about us, an' we'd be Lunnon folks ourselves. ' An',' says he, ' we'll have the crops
brought to ruin an' the game drove off an' everythin' murked up wi' black soot an' cinders.' "

This troubled the Hawthorn Tree very much. It knew very little of London, because it had been so bound down by circumstances that it had not travelled, but somehow the things it had heard of the great city had given it a terror of it. It regarded it as a great black monster doing only harm; starving poor people; making rich people careless, and worldly, and selfish; harboring thieves, and poisoning the pure air with its smoky breath. This was not altogether a just opinion, but then the Hawthorn Tree had lived a very quiet, limited life; an innocent, pure, country life, but not a life in which it could learn how to look at all sides of a subject. But it had this good quality, however, the simple country Hawthorn Tree, it was not obstinate, and set in its opinions; it was inexperienced and ignorant in some ways, but it was not so ignorant as to think it knew everything. This is an ignorance people do not recover from.

But it was very much afraid of London, and indeed time proved that it had reason to be. And it passed through many sorrows. The years passed by—a great many years—and as each year passed, the dark cloud overhanging London town crept nearer and nearer, and the sky, which had always before been fair and clear, began to look as if its blue were dulled. More than this, the Hawthorn Tree could see not only the dark pall of smoke, but the chimneys themselves which poured it forth. Not only the chimneys of houses, but tall chimneys of factories of all kinds, from which volumes of blackness rolled all day, and sometimes, it seemed, all night.

Everything changed again and again as the years went by; the people changed the fashion of the clothes they wore, their very speech itself. Oh, the Hawthorn Tree saw many sad, and many gay, and many interesting things. The Squire who had tasted the smoke in his tankard of ale died, and his son and heir got into debt and sold his estate, and the trees were cut down and the estate cut up into small pieces for building houses upon. And the smoke and chimneys kept coming nearer and nearer, and the air was not so fresh as it had been, and the people that passed oftenest were not rosy country farmers and their wives, but sometimes richly-dressed people who dashed by in fine carriages, and poorly-dressed ones who had pale faces, and who often looked hungry and tired. They were all going either to or from great London, and the Hawthorn Tree saw them all, and often used to scatter its blossoms over the pale ones, and sigh so with all its leaves, that sometimes they would look up and think the wind had risen. "Oh, great London," the Hawthorn Tree was whispering; "oh, great, busy, sorrowful, dark London, do not come

18

nearer; do not, do not." But great London was too busy to hear. There was too great a whirl in its streets, the carts and carriages and wagons were rumbling over its stones, people were hurrying to and fro; there was so much noise and pleasure, and business and sorrow, how could the far-off, sorrowful rustle of one poor Hawthorn Tree make itself heard?

Then there came a cruel day for the Hawthorn Tree.

It had noticed that not far from it—in a place it could quite easily see—something was being built—a large building. Men were at work constantly. At length it began to grow taller in one part than in another, much taller.

One day at noon some men passed, talking.

"The factory's chimney is going on," said one.

"Yes," said the other, "they expect to finish it and set to work soon," and they went their way.

"It is a chimney," said the Hawthorn Tree, "a factory chimney!"

It was just putting out its first blossoms, and those that opened that day had no pink on them at all, they were quite white.

By the time the tree was in full bloom the factory chimney was finished, and then it began work. How the black smoke rolled out, and darkened the blue sky and touched the edges of the fleecy, snow-white little young clouds with dingy yellow.

And, alas! it was not long before the Hawthorn Tree felt something begin to fall lightly on its blossoms, on its fresh snow-white and pink innocent blossoms; its lovely, tender, fragrant blossoms.

"What is it?" it cried, trembling. "It is black, and like very small flakes of black snow." Then the cruel truth flashed upon it.

"It is soot!" it cried.

The Hawthorn Tree burst into tears.

"There is a great deal of dew this morning," said some one who stood under the branches.

Once, many years before, one of the many people from whom the tree gained its information, one of those who rested in its shade, had told to some children a story. It was about a great black dragon which swallowed up everything beautiful that came in its way, and left behind it in its track only desolation and dust and ashes.

How often the Hawthorn Tree thought of the story in the years that came after the soot first fell on its blossoms. Great London was the dragon. How it crept onward, how it swallowed up the green fields, the flowers, the trees, the hedges with the birds' nests in them, the clean, country roads, the cottages with thatched roofs and diamond-paned windows, with tiny white curtains and flower pots in them. How it swallowed up the fresh, rosy children, and their games and laughter. And in its track it left hundreds of dingy houses, hundreds of tall chimneys, hundreds of black, close, ugly streets, thousands of pale, hungry-looking people, some with worn-out faces, some with cunning, evil ones; some simply dull and brutal.

It was not the rich and gay part of London which had crawled out to the Hawthorn Tree and beyond it; if it had been so, perhaps the tree might not have feared and hated it so and called it a dragon. It might then have had quite a different idea, and have been delighted with the bright luminous world it would have seen, with the carriages and horses, the beautiful women and pretty children. But it was only the wretched, squalid part the Hawthorn Tree saw. And after a long time, when its heart was almost broken, and it really thought things could not be any worse, it found out that it lived in what was called the East End, and in one of the worst and most crowded parts of it.

It was a long time, too long for the Hawthorn Tree to calculate the months and years before the worst came to the worst, and before all the air was thick with stifling smoke and unhealthy odors; before the miserable houses had huddled themselves together into wretched, filthy streets,

where wretched, filthy people starved, and quarrelled, and fought, and suffered, and died, where
little children cursed each other as they played,
in their rags, in the gutters, where their drunken
mothers staggered and fell on the pavement or
on the steps of the noisome houses, and slept
their horrible besotted sleep. There were alley-
ways and courts where decent people dared not
go in the broad day, and in the dreadful rooms
were packed together drunkards and thieves, and
sometimes murderers hiding from justice.

And, oh, the hunger and the pain and the helplessness of the little ones born there! The Hawthorn Tree used to tremble at the sight of them,
more than at the sight of the great, heavy, brutal
men who lounged about or crept stealthily round
corners or bandied coarse jokes with each other.
They had such pale, cunning, old little faces, such
stunted bodies, such unchildish ways when they
played or fought together. They were, most of
them, used to oaths and lies, and tricks, and
abuse; the first they were not troubled by, the
last they were sharp at slipping out of the way
of. They were all alike in one thing, however—
they all liked the Hawthorn Tree, black and
scanty-leaved and unlike itself as its troubles
had made it.

"Oh, if I could only blossom for them!" it
used to sigh.

But its blossoms had grown fewer and fewer every spring from the first; they could not live in the poisoned air, and at last there had come a spring when there had been none at all, and from that time the Hawthorn was a hopelessly sorrowful tree, and if it had not had a kind heart, it would have died itself. But it struggled on in the midst of the dirt and misery, though it could not put forth as many leaves as it used to, and some of its branches died. The truth was that it had been led to make the struggle through a very sad, simple story.

One morning there had staggered and fallen under its poor shade a little shuddering, sobbing child, such a thin, white-faced little thing, with such a woeful look in its hungry blue eyes, and with the marks of cruel stripes and bruises showing through its rags. It lay and sobbed and shivered until the Hawthorn shivered too, and at last, because it could do nothing else, dropped two or three of its leaves upon its cheek. The child moved, and, by chance, the little leaves fell into its hand. Who knows but that all the Hawthorn's wishing and sympathy had given the poor little leaves some touch of the magic charm of love?

The child looked at them through her tears; the rain had washed them to a fresher green than usual, and to a child who had never seen the country grass and flowers, they seemed so pretty. After she had looked at them a few minutes, she stopped crying, then she sat up and began to scratch at the earth with her fingers. The tree wondered if she were going to make dirt pies, but she was not. She made little squares of the soft dirt, and stuck the stems of the leaves in them. Perhaps sometimes she had wandered far enough into the better part of the city to see a square or garden, and she was trying to make something like it. She busied herself over it, and changed it again and again ; it was more to her than a few tiny squares of dust and a few leaves ; it was a new interest which actually filled her mind so that she forgot her sorrows. Did she know that the Hawthorn Tree was watching her and whispering, " Poor child, poor child ! " She felt some comfort about her at all events, and suddenly she put her arms round the trunk of the tree and rested her sorrowful, thin cheek against it, and looked up in the branches, and smiled as if at a friend.

" I mustn't die," said the Hawthorn Tree tearfully to itself when at last she went away. " It is quite plain that I mustn't die. The — the children need me, even though I can't blossom." It would have been cut down without doubt, but that it chanced to stand on a small square of ground whose owners were rich and unbusiness-

like enough to forget that it belonged to them.
At one time there had been a sort of wooden
fencing about this piece of ground, but this had
rotted and broken and fallen away here and
there, so that there were gaps in it, and anyone
who wished could make his way in and out.

Because it was neglected and seemed to belong
to no one, as the neighborhood became worse
and worse, this enclosure became such a hideous
prison for the poor Hawthorn Tree as would in
the end have been its death if rescue had not
come. But I must tell you how this came about.
In the dreadful houses in the filthy narrow streets
and courts the people who were herded together
often had wretched refuse they wished to throw
away. A cat died, a dog, it was easy to throw
them over the rotten palings into the enclosure;
a poor creature had fever or small-pox, and the
mattress on which she had died must be disposed
of. So, one dark night, it was bundled up and
thrown into the enclosure to lie there, rotted by
the rain and sun, and beaten into chaff by the
wind, which scattered its seeds of plague in the
air. Drunken men and women used to stagger
into the enclosure to wrangle and fight and fall
into stupid sleep. Thieves used to meet there to
talk over their plans; often desperate brawls
arose which ended in the flash of a knife in the
air or the thud of a bludgeon, and awful oaths

and cries which brought policemen and people running together. Once there was found among the loathsome weeds the striped dress of a convict who had escaped and changed his clothes here, so that he might not be recognized.

The Hawthorn Tree remembered the night this had happened. It had been a dark, sultry night, and the first thing the tree noticed was a stealthy, shuffling sound as if someone were making his way through a gap in the side of the board fencing which was left standing; then heavy limping feet had dragged over the ground; there had been the sound of hoarse, panting breathing, which had drawn nearer and nearer till the breather stood beneath the Hawthorn Tree, and then, with a stifled oath, he dropped, threw himself on the earth, and leaned his back against the trunk.

"It's dark enough 'ere," he said; "an' I shan't have no bull's-eye lanterns a-flashin' in an' disturbin' of me. They're not fond of this 'ere corner, them blokes. They leaves it to itself; I shall have a chance to change these 'ere togs for them I nipped from that chap as 'ad fell asleep on his tramp. They ain't swell, but they're less conspikyus than them I'm wearin'."

He changed his convict's dress for the poor things he had stolen, and then limped painfully away. He had hurt his leg in making his escape;

it was said the next day when his things were
found that there were spots of blood on some of
them.

"Strange people sit under me in these days,"
sighed the Hawthorn Tree, "and somehow I
can't help feeling sad for them all—even the bad
ones. Perhaps they can't be good ones when
they live here and never breathe the fresh air
or see anything blossom."

But not long after this it found out that there
were some who lived there who were good, but it
was also true that they had often breathed the
fresh air and seen things blossom.

Not far from the loathsome, barren plot of
ground where the Hawthorn Tree lived its sad
life there was a church. It was an old church;
so old that in its records there were the deaths of
some of the first people who had died in the
Great Plague of London hundreds of years before. It was not a beautiful church, and certainly
not a fashionable one; but it had a rector, and his
rectory was a quaint house across the street, only
a short distance from the Hawthorn Tree. It
might not be considered a very enviable thing to
be the rector of this East-end parish, but the rector and his young wife were people with strong
and warm hearts, and found their hands and time
full of things to interest them and keep them
busy. It would be very easy to write a whole

book full of the things they found to do and did, but I have time to tell only one thing, how they became friends of the Hawthorn Tree and saved it from death and despair. The tree had seen the rector often as he passed, and had noticed how different his keen, handsome face was from those of the other people who went by. It was the face of a gentleman, and though the Hawthorn Tree did not know what a gentleman was, it could see the differences in the faces.

"He must have breathed the pure air. He must have seen things blossom," was the vague thought in its tree heart.

There was always a crowd of rough, brutal men about the corner of the uncared-for piece of ground. As there was nothing built upon it and it seemed to belong to nobody, the worst of the bad and idle ones got into the habit of lounging, smoking, and quarrelling there, and even the policemen avoided it. Drunken fellows staggered and squabbled, shouted and maundered there, lads played pitch and toss, thieves bandied jokes about their spoils, and met to plot and talk their plans over. The place was so given over to roystering noise and evil that the more decent people felt it unsafe to pass it.

"The place is an eyesore and a horror," the rector said, looking across the street from his study window. "Every pestilential thing is thrown into it to poison the air; that is bad enough to begin with, and the plague that gathers about that corner is the worst of all. Something ought to be done."

He and his wife often said something ought to be done, but it seemed impossible to say what could be done. The poisonous odors of the rotting garbage which was thrown over the remnant of tottering, decaying palings made their way across the street to the rectory, and the riotous groups with their oaths and foul words made it necessary often to keep the windows closed.

"That poor old Hawthorn Tree," said the rector's wife one day, "what a horrible, desolate life for it! The wonder is that it did not die long ago. And yet it struggles to put out a few green leaves every year."

"It is marvellous that any green thing can live there," said the rector. "One often wonders at the courage of the poor bits of plants that somehow manage to live and feebly bloom in their rough pots or boxes in the windows of some poor child or woman living in one room up a wretched court."

One might also fancy that they had souls, and longed to give their bit of brightness as a sort of comfort to the miserable lives.

The rector looked very thoughtful. He knew

those wretched courts and miserable lives so well.

"If that unholy spot," he said, "could be cleansed, fenced in, and given up to the poor old Hawthorn Tree to die peaceably in — or, if the poor thing might live, and even have some other humble green thing near it—how it would purify the whole street."

He ended the words almost with a start, as if some sudden thought had struck him.

"That they should even see some simple fresh thing putting forth its leaves and growing in their midst would be a good thing," he said, "if it could only be—ah, if!"

And this was the beginning of the Hawthorn Tree's new life — these few sentences which awakened a bold thought in the rector's mind —a thought which ripened into a bold plan. And the rector was not a man to make a plan, and then not work hard to make it a reality. The Hawthorn Tree did not know any of the details, and would not have dared even to hope for what afterwards came to pass ; it did not know how the rector's thought took shape, and how in a few days he was hard at work developing his plan, and taking his first steps, how he went to see this man and that, and talked to each of them in deepest earnestness of his poor East-end parish, and the suffering and hopelessness and crime in it; of the people who starved and stifled in their dreadful streets and alleys; of the little children who lived through their helpless childhood without one innocent childish pleasure or joy, who never saw grass or flowers or trees growing, being so far from the public parks and so uncared for. And then he told of the loathsome plot of ground and the harmful rubbish thrown on it, and the odors and infection poisoning the air. He could tell them what a death-trap and rendezvous of criminals it had become, of the foul-mouthed, riotous crowd always at the corner, of its desertion by the police, who felt they had nothing to do with it, and of the murderous fights that went on at night under cover of the broken palings.

And then he told them of his plan, and when they smiled at it as impossible, he was not discouraged. There were some who did not smile, but, being moved by his eloquence and earnestness, listened with interest, and asked questions and promised their help.

So a few months afterwards the Hawthorn Tree saw a new thing happen. The rector came over with some workmen, and these workmen began to clear away the heaps of filth and rubbish from the piece of ground, and after this had been done they roughly, but strongly, repaired the tumble-down fence, so that people could not pass through the gaps.

"Can it be that someone has bought the grounds?" said the Hawthorn Tree. "No one would want it except to build another dreadful factory on, with another tall chimney to pour forth smoke. They will cut me down before they do anything else; but I do not care," it added with a sigh, "I am stifling to death, I cannot blossom, even my leaves are going, and children cannot come to play under me now."

But it seemed that no one was going to cut it down at once, whether the factory were built or not, and it could not help noticing that, at least, the air was better and the place quieter. For some reason the policemen began to take notice of the corner and use their authority when there was any loitering about or tendency to disorder.

The bad characters who had used it as a rendezvous found they must keep away; there was no more foul language, no more pitch and toss, there were no more drunken fights.

"I am glad of that, whatever happens," thought the Hawthorn Tree.

And at last—but it was after the rector had worked very hard indeed in all sorts of ways— there came a day when more workmen arrived and began to work in such a way as made the Hawthorn Tree quite sure its last hour had come. They began to dig in the hard beaten earth, they dug deep into it with picks and broke it with spades.

"But why don't they cut me down first?" said the poor sad tree; "surely they have forgotten me, and they will do it soon."

The second day the rector came into the ground and stood among them, talking and giving orders, and at last he turned round.

"Loosen the earth well around the roots of that old tree; I want to give it a chance to live," he said. "It has held its own bravely enough, poor old thing. If it lives, it will be the first tree in the garden."

"The garden," said the Hawthorn Tree, "a garden; oh! what does he mean? A chance to live! I am not to be cut down! What are they going to do?"

It found a reason for living, as it looked on day after day and listened and learned about the rector's plan.

It took time to carry it out, a time long enough to allow much work to be done, to allow grass to grow, young trees and flowers to be planted and thrive, paths to be laid out, and such things to be accomplished as the Hawthorn Tree could not have believed could ever be done.

For the rector had worked until he had managed with the aid of those who listened without laughing at his plan, and indeed with the aid of some who had smiled at first, to get possession of the deserted ground which had been a place so awful and worse than desolate. And with the aid of time and wonderful energy and planning he had transformed it into a fresh, sweet, blooming, restful place, where the brown sparrows twittered, and all sorts of green and bright things grew, and the little children who had never seen such things before came in to wander about and watch them growing day by day, and wonder at and delight in them. And the rector called it the People's Garden.

It seemed almost incredible that such a thing could be in such a place, and be so fresh and bloom and thrive so well. But the rector knew what simple brave things would grow even in East-end London air, and he had such things planted. There were no rare things, but they were all rare to the poor people and the children who lived in the alleys and courts. There was thick green grass, where daisies and buttercups actually grew; there were pretty humble flowers, and bushes, and small trees; there was even a little irregular pond made to look quite like a sort of stream, and fresh-water plants grew in it, and there was a little fountain to cool and clear the air. And on this the rector had one or two model ships and boats for the sake of the children, who, seeing them, would have something to examine

19

and think of. And there was a cool, deep grotto, built of pieces of rock, and out of its crevices ferns and creeping plants sprang; and there were seats where people could rest in the shade and freshness and be quiet. It was wonderful how much was made of that one piece of ground, and how almost impossible it seemed when one was in it that this greenness, and sweetness, and calm could be in the East-end of London, and only a short distance from the most dreadful places. It sweetened and purified all the air about it, and surely it sweetened and purified the poor lives of those who came to it.

" It is for the people," said the rector, " for the tired ones, and those who are ill, and for the mothers and children."

And the poor old Hawthorn Tree's almost broken heart was healed.

From the first the rector had felt tenderly towards it, and had tried to help it to live. One of the first things done was to wash off with the hose its poor trunk and branches and leaves, to free them from the years of smoke, and soot, and dust. The ground about it was taken care of, and it was encouraged in every way the rector and the gardener could think of. And when it felt and saw the grass growing about its feet, and leaves and buds putting forth, a thrill went through its every fibre and it gained new strength. And one day in the spring two little country birds who had lost themselves fluttered and twittered in one of its boughs.

"One might build a nest here if there were more leaves," one of them chirped. "It's very strange to find the country here. I think it must be the country. We might be quite safe."

"Oh, I shall have more leaves," trembled the Hawthorn Tree, though they did not understand it. "I am so happy that I feel sure I shall have more leaves, and perhaps, oh, perhaps, I shall even blossom."

And as the days became warmer it did begin to have more leaves, more and more every day, until the birds began to fly to it whenever they wanted to twitter and rest and preen their feathers, and the rector, passing by one day with his wife, stood beneath it and looked up with a pleased smile.

"See how the old Hawthorn Tree has flourished," he said. "It has grown quite young again. And there—why, my dear, there are some blossoms! How delighted the children will be to see them! The little lame boy told me, the other day, he had never seen a tree with flowers on it." And he laid his hand on its rough bark quite tenderly.

"I am so happy," whispered the Hawthorn Tree. "The birds rest in my branches, and the

grass and all the flowers and leaves are my friends ;
even the little flags and water reeds in the little
lake whisper and rustle kind things to me. And
the little children play about me until their faces
are quite bright. Oh, I am glad I tried to live ;
I am happy again."

The rector did not hear, of course. He thought
a little breeze was passing, and he lifted his hat
to enjoy its coolness.

"I think I shall put one of the seats under it,"
he said ; "the children are so fond of it, they are
always clustering about it."

And he had the seats put there, and I have seen
them, for, as I have written at the head of the
page, this is the Quite True Story of a Hawthorn Tree ; at least, I think it is the story the
Hawthorn Tree would tell if it could speak.
The rector took me, not so long ago, and showed
me his beautiful, wonderful, little People's Garden, and, as we walked about the paths and
looked at the fresh, bravely-growing flowers and
bushes and plants, he told me how horrible a
place it had once been, and how he had formed
the plan to rescue and transform it from a hideous plague-spot gathering all evil and loathsome
things about it, to a quiet, bright nook, where the
poor people could come and find beautiful, simple
nature, even in their dirty East - end. And he
showed me the shaded seats and the bath-chairs,

of which he had two or three, so that the ill and helpless ones might be brought from their stifling garrets and cellars, and drawn to the dear little garden and rest there, and breathe the purer air and watch the leaves moved by the summer wind. And it was then he showed me the Hawthorn Tree, and told me it had been there since there had been fields about it, and all through the long years when it was surrounded only by heaps of filth and garbage. And I could not help but love and pity it.

"Ah," I said, "how happy it must be, and how surprised to find the grass growing about it again! It must feel as if it were once more in the country. What sorrowful years it must have lived through, and what a story it could tell! I wish it could tell it to me!"

And as I did not know the tree language, and it could not tell it to me, I tried to tell it to myself, and so I have tried to tell it to you.

Charles Scribner's Sons'

New and Standard Books for
Young Readers for 1897=98...

MRS. BURNETT'S
FAMOUS JUVENILES

An entirely new edition of Mrs. Burnett's famous juveniles from new plates, with all the original illustrations. Bound in a beautiful new cloth binding designed by R. B. Birch, and sold at very much reduced prices.

LITTLE LORD FAUNTLEROY
TWO LITTLE PILGRIMS' PROGRESS
SARA CREWE and LITTLE SAINT ELIZABETH AND
    OTHER STORIES (in one vol.)
PICCINO AND OTHER CHILD STORIES
GIOVANNI AND THE OTHER

Five Volumes, 12mo, each, $1.25

The original editions can still be supplied at the former prices:

LITTLE LORD FAUNTLEROY. Beautifully illustrated by REGINALD B. BIRCH. Square 8vo, $2.00.

TWO LITTLE PILGRIMS' PROGRESS. A STORY OF THE CITY BEAUTIFUL. By Mrs. FRANCES HODGSON BURNETT. Illustrated by REGINALD B. BIRCH. Uniform with "Fauntleroy," etc. Square 8vo, $1.50.

SARA CREWE; OR, WHAT HAPPENED AT MISS MINCHIN'S. Richly and fully illustrated by REGINALD B. BIRCH. Square 8vo, $1.00.

LITTLE SAINT ELIZABETH, AND OTHER STORIES. With 12 full-page drawings by REGINALD B. BIRCH. Square 8vo, $1.50.

GIOVANNI AND THE OTHER: CHILDREN WHO HAVE MADE STORIES. With 9 full-page illustrations by REGINALD B. BIRCH. Square 8vo, $1.50.

PICCINO, AND OTHER CHILD STORIES. Fully illustrated by REGINALD B. BIRCH. Square 8vo, $1.50.

G. A. HENTY'S POPULAR STORIES FOR BOYS

New Volumes for 1897-98. Each, crown 8vo, handsomely illustrated, $1.50.

Mr. Henty, the most popular writer of Books of Adventure in England, adds three new volumes to his list this fall—books that will delight thousands of boys on this side who have become his ardent admirers

WITH FREDERICK THE GREAT. A TALE OF THE SEVEN YEARS' WAR. With 12 full-page illustrations. 12mo, $1.50.

This story, more than any other of Mr. Henty's, follows closely the historic lines, and no better description of the memorable battles of Rossbach, Leuthen, Prague, Zorndorf, Hochkirch, and Torgau can be found anywhere than is given in this volume. Through the historic part there runs the record of the daring and hazardous adventures of the hero, so that the charm of romance is given to the whole narrative. It is one of the most important volumes Mr. Henty has written.

A MARCH ON LONDON. A STORY OF WAT TYLER'S RISING. With 8 full-page illustrations by W. H. MARGETSON. 12mo, $1.50.

This book weaves together, in a most interesting way, the story of Wat Tyler's rebellion under King Richard, the civil war in Flanders which occurred soon after, and the ill-planned attack upon the French led by the Bishop of Norfolk. The whole story is singularly interesting, covering as it does a period of history which is but little known and which is well worth narrating.

WITH MOORE AT CORUNNA. A STORY OF THE PENINSULAR WAR. With 12 full-page illustrations by WAL. PAGET. 12mo, $1.50.

A bright Irish lad, Terence O'Connor, is living with his widowed father, Captain O'Connor of the Mayo Fusiliers, with the regiment, at the time when the Peninsular War against Napoleon began. Under the command of Sir John Moore, he shared in the same marching and sharp fighting which that expedition experienced up to the battle of Corunna. By his bravery and great usefulness, in spite of his youth, he received a commission as colonel in the Portuguese army, and during the remainder of the war rendered great services, being mentioned twice in the general orders of the Duke of Wellington. The whole story is full of exciting military experiences and gives a most careful and accurate account of the conduct of the campaigns.

MR. HENTY'S OTHER BOOKS

Each volume with numerous illustrations; handsomely bound. Olivine edges. 12mo. $1.50.

"Mr. Henty's books never fail to interest boy readers. Among writers of stories of adventure he stands in the very first rank."—*Academy*, London.

"No country nor epoch of history is there which Mr. Henty does not know, and what is really remarkable is that he always writes well and interestingly. Boys like stirring adventures, and Mr. Henty is a master of this method of composition."—*New York Times*.

AT AGINCOURT. A Tale of the White Hoods of Paris. With 12 full-page illustrations by WAL. PAGET.

COCHRANE THE DAUNTLESS. A Tale of the Exploits of Lord Cochrane in South American Waters. With 12 full-page illustrations by W. H. MARGETSON.

ON THE IRRAWADDY. A Story of the First Burmese War. With 8 full-page illustrations by W. H. OVEREND.

THROUGH RUSSIAN SNOWS. A Story of Napoleon's Retreat from Moscow. With 8 full-page illustrations by W. H. OVEREND.

A KNIGHT OF THE WHITE CROSS. A Tale of the Siege of Rhodes. With 12 full-page illustrations by RALPH PEACOCK.

THE TIGER OF MYSORE. A Story of the War with Tippoo Said. With 12 full-page illustrations by W. H. MARGETSON.

IN THE HEART OF THE ROCKIES. A Story of Adventure in Colorado.

WHEN LONDON BURNED. A Story of Restoration Times and the Great Fire.

WULF THE SAXON. A Story of the Norman Conquest.

ST. BARTHOLOMEW'S EVE. A Tale of the Huguenot Wars.

THROUGH THE SIKH WAR. A Tale of the Conquest of the Punjaub.

A JACOBITE EXILE. Being the Adventures of a Young Englishman in the Service of Charles XII. of Sweden.

CONDEMNED AS A NIHILIST. A Story of Escape from Siberia.

BERIC THE BRITON. A Story of the Roman Invasion.

IN GREEK WATERS. A Story of the Grecian War of Independence [1821–1827].

THE DASH FOR KHARTOUM. A Tale of the Nile Expedition.

REDSKIN AND COWBOY. A Tale of the Western Plains.

HELD FAST FOR ENGLAND. A Tale of the Siege of Gibraltar.

SOME OF THE NEWEST BOOKS

WILL SHAKESPEARE'S LITTLE LAD. By IMOGEN CLARK. With illustrations and cover design by R. B. Birch. 12mo, $1.50.

A story, full of warm color and brisk movement, of Stratford life in Shakespeare's day, the local atmosphere being reflected with rare fidelity, and the hero, the poet's son, being drawn with sympathy and charm.

CHILD POEMS. By EUGENE FIELD. With an introduction by KENNETH GRAHAME and profusely illustrated by CHARLES ROBINSON. Uniform with Robert Louis Stevenson's "Child's Garden of Verses," also illustrated by Charles Robinson. 12mo, $1.50.

THE STEVENSON SONG BOOK. VERSES FROM "A CHILD'S GARDEN," by ROBERT LOUIS STEVENSON. With music by various composers. A companion volume to the Field-DeKoven song book printed last year. Large 8vo, $2.00.

AN OLD-FIELD SCHOOL GIRL. By MARION HARLAND. With 8 full-page illustrations. 12mo, $1.25.

LORDS OF THE WORLD. By ALFRED J. CHURCH. A STORY OF THE FALL OF CARTHAGE AND CORINTH. With 12 full-page illustrations by RALPH PEACOCK. 12mo, $1.50.

The scene of this story centres in the overthrow and destruction of Carthage by the Romans. The story is full of valuable historical details and the interest never flags.

HEROES OF OUR NAVY. By MOLLY ELLIOT SEAWELL. Illustrated. 12mo. *In press.*

Never has this entertaining writer been more felicitous than in the present volume.

THE LAST CRUISE OF THE MOHAWK. By W. J. HENDERSON. Illustrated by HARRY EDWARDS. 12mo, $1.25.

The book is crowded with dramatic incident — mutiny, shipwreck, Farragut's great fight in Mobile Bay — and the narrative is as simple as the events and characters are entertaining.

KIRK MUNROE'S STIRRING TALES

THE WHITE CONQUEROR SERIES

WITH CROCKETT AND BOWIE	AT WAR WITH PONTIAC
THE WHITE CONQUERORS	THROUGH SWAMP AND GLADE

Each, illustrated, 12mo, $1.25.   The complete set, 4 vols., in a box, $5.00.

JUST PUBLISHED

WITH CROCKETT AND BOWIE; OR, FIGHTING FOR THE LONE STAR FLAG. A TALE OF TEXAS. With 8 full-page illustrations by VICTOR PÉRARD.

The story is of the Texas revolution in 1835, when American Texans under Sam Houston, Bowie, Crockett, and Travis, fought for relief from the intolerable tyranny of the Mexican Santa Aña. The hero, Rex Hardin, son of a Texas ranchman, and graduate of an American military school, takes a prominent part in the heroic defense of the Alamo, the terrible scenes at Goliad, and the final triumph at San Jacinto. The historical side of the story has been carefully studied and its localities rendered familiar by a special trip to Texas undertaken by the author for that purpose within a year.

PREVIOUS VOLUMES

THROUGH SWAMP AND GLADE. A TALE OF THE SEMINOLE WAR. With 8 full-page illustrations by VICTOR PÉRARD. 12mo, $1.25.

In this new story Mr. Munroe opens to view an exceedingly interesting period of American history—the period of the Seminole War in Florida. Coacoochee, the hero of the story, is a young Indian of noble birth, the son of Philip, the chieftain of the Seminoles. He is a boy at the time of the beginning of the Seminole troubles and grows up to lead his tribe in the long struggle which resulted in the Indians being driven from the north of Florida down to the distant southern wilderness. It is full of strange adventure, of stirring incident and rapid action, and it is a true and faithful picture of a period of history little known to young readers.

AT WAR WITH PONTIAC; OR, THE TOTEM OF THE BEAR. A TALE OF RED-COAT AND REDSKIN. With 8 full-page illustrations by J. FINNEMORE. 12mo, $1.25.

A story of old days in America when Detroit was a frontier town and the shores of Lake Erie were held by hostile Indians under Pontiac. The hero, Donald Hester, goes in search of his sister Edith, who has been captured by the Indians. Strange and terrible are his experiences; for he is wounded, taken prisoner, condemned to be burned, and contrives to escape. In the end there is peace between Pontiac and the English, and all things terminate happily for the hero. One dares not skip a page of this enthralling story.

THE WHITE CONQUERORS. A TALE OF TOLTEC AND AZTEC. With 8 full-page illustrations by W. S. STACEY. 12mo, $1.25.

This story deals with the Conquest of Mexico by Cortes and his Spaniards, the "White Conquerors," who, after many deeds of valor, pushed their way into the great Aztec kingdom and established their power in the wondrous city where Montezuma reigned in barbaric splendor.

BOOKS BY WILLIAM HENRY FROST

JUST PUBLISHED

THE KNIGHTS OF THE ROUND TABLE. Illustrated and cover designed by
S. R. BURLEIGH. 12mo, $1.50.

Mr. Frost's volumes of folk-lore stories have achieved a deserved popularity, and
this last one, dealing with the ever-fascinating theme of the Round Table and its
knights, is equal to either of his earlier books.

MR. FROST'S FORMER BOOKS

THE COURT OF KING ARTHUR. STORIES FROM THE LAND OF THE ROUND
TABLE. Illustrated by S. R. BURLEIGH. 12mo, $1.50.

Mr. Frost has had the happy idea of making a journey to the different places connected with the Arthurian romances by history or legend, and of relating the ever
new Round Table Tales on their sites, to the same little girl, now somewhat older,
to whom he told his charming Wagner stories.

THE WAGNER STORY BOOK. FIRELIGHT TALES OF THE GREAT MUSIC
DRAMAS. Illustrated by SIDNEY R. BURLEIGH. 12mo, $1.50.

"A successful attempt to make the romantic themes of the music drama intelligi-
ble to young readers. The author has full command of his subject, and the style
is easy, graceful, and simple."—*Boston Beacon.*

ROBERT GRANT'S TWO BOOKS FOR BOYS

JACK HALL; OR, THE SCHOOL DAYS OF AN AMERICAN BOY. Illustrated by F.
G. ATTWOOD. 12mo, $1.25.

"A better book for boys has never been written. It is pure, clean, and healthy,
and has throughout a vigorous action that holds the reader breathlessly."
—*Boston Herald.*

JACK IN THE BUSH; OR, A SUMMER ON A SALMON RIVER. Illustrated by F. T.
MERRILL. 12mo, $1.25.

"A clever book for boys. It is the story of the camp life of a lot of boys, and is
destined to please every boy reader. It is attractively illustrated."
—*Detroit Free Press.*

THE KANTER GIRLS

By MARY L. B. BRANCH. Illustrated by HELEN M. ARMSTRONG. Square 12mo,
$1.50.

The adventures of Jane and Prue, two small sisters, among different peoples of
the imaginative world—dryads, snow-children, Kobolds, etc.—aided by their
invisible rings, their magic boat, and their wonderful birds, are described by the
author with great naturalness and a true gift for story-telling. The numerous
illustrations are very attractive, and in thorough sympathy with the text.

SAMUEL ADAMS DRAKE'S HISTORICAL BOOKS

JUST ISSUED

THE BORDER WARS OF NEW ENGLAND

COMMONLY CALLED KING WILLIAM'S AND QUEEN ANNE'S WARS. By SAMUEL ADAMS DRAKE. With 58 illustrations and maps. 12mo, $1.50.

Mr. Drake has made a consecutive, entertaining narrative of the border wars which the French and Indians waged against the English settlers in New England during the reigns of King William and Queen Anne. The story is full of adventurous interest and is told with that minute attention to suggestive and instructive details which have been the distinguishing feature of Mr. Drake's other books. The illustrations, many of them from photographs of historic spots and of buildings still standing, are of exceptional interest.

FORMER VOLUMES

THE MAKING OF THE OHIO VALLEY STATES. 1660-1837. Illustrated. 12mo, $1.50.

THE MAKING OF VIRGINIA AND THE MIDDLE COLONIES. 1578-1701. Illustrated. 12mo, $1.50.

THE MAKING OF NEW ENGLAND. 1580-1643. With 148 illustrations and with maps. 12mo, $1.50.

THE MAKING OF THE GREAT WEST. 1812-1853. With 145 illustrations and with maps. 12mo, $1.50.

STORIES OF LITERATURE, SCIENCE, AND HISTORY BY HENRIETTA CHRISTIAN WRIGHT

A NEW VOLUME JUST ISSUED

CHILDREN'S STORIES IN AMERICAN LITERATURE.—1860-1896. 12mo, $1.25.

Miss Wright here continues the attractive presentation of literary history begun in her "Children's Stories in English Literature," taking up the literary figures that have appeared since the time of the civil war, and treating their works and personalities in a simple manner, interesting to young readers.

CHILDREN'S STORIES IN AMERICAN LITERATURE.—1660-1860. 12mo, $1.25.

CHILDREN'S STORIES IN ENGLISH LITERATURE. Two volumes: TALIESIN TO SHAKESPEARE—SHAKESPEARE TO TENNYSON. 12mo, each, $1.25.

CHILDREN'S STORIES OF THE GREAT SCIENTISTS. With portraits. 12mo, $1.25.

CHILDREN'S STORIES IN AMERICAN HISTORY. Illustrated. 12mo, $1.25.

CHILDREN'S STORIES OF AMERICAN PROGRESS. Illustrated. 12mo, $1.25.

THREE BOOKS OF SPORTS AND GAMES

THE AMERICAN BOY'S BOOK OF SPORT. OUT-DOOR GAMES FOR ALL SEASONS. By DANIEL C. BEARD. With over 300 illustrations by the author. 8vo, $2.50.

This is an entirely new book by Mr. Beard, containing altogether new matter of great interest to all young lovers of sport. It is a companion volume to the author's well-known "American Boy's Handy Book," of which over twenty-five thousand copies have been sold, and will undoubtedly rival that famous work in popularity as it does in interest.

THE AMERICAN BOY'S HANDY BOOK; OR, WHAT TO DO AND HOW TO DO IT. By DANIEL C. BEARD. With 360 illustrations by the author. Square 8vo, $2.00.

" The book has this great advantage over its predecessors, that most of the games, tricks, and other amusements described in it are new. It treats of sports adapted to all seasons of the year ; it is practical, and it is well illustrated."
—*New York Tribune.*

THE AMERICAN GIRL'S HANDY BOOK. By LENA and ADELIA B. BEARD. With over 500 illustrations by the authors. Square 8vo, $2.00.

"I have put it in my list of good and useful books for young people, as I have many requests for advice from my little friends and their anxious mothers. I am most happy to commend your very ingenious and entertaining book."
—LOUISA M. ALCOTT.

THOMAS NELSON PAGE'S TWO BOOKS

AMONG THE CAMPS; OR, YOUNG PEOPLE'S STORIES OF THE WAR. With 8 full-page illustrations. Square 8vo, $1.50.

" They are five in number, each having reference to some incident of the Civil War. A vein of mingled pathos and humor runs through them all, and greatly heightens the charm of them. It is the early experience of the author himself, doubtless, which makes his pictures of life in a Southern home during the great struggle so vivid and truthful."—*The Nation.*

TWO LITTLE CONFEDERATES. With 8 full-page illustrations by KEMBLE and REDWOOD. Square 8vo, $1.50.

" Mr. Page was 'raised' in Virginia, and he knows the 'darkey' of the South better than any one who writes about them. And he knows 'white folks,' too, and his stories, whether for old or young people, have the charm of sincerity and beauty and reality."—*Harper's Young People.*

EDWARD EGGLESTON'S TWO POPULAR BOOKS

THE HOOSIER SCHOOL-BOY. Illustrated. 12mo, $1.00.

" 'The Hoosier School-Boy' depicts some of the characteristics of boy-life years ago on the Ohio ; characteristics, however, that were not peculiar to that section. The story presents a vivid and interesting picture of the difficulties which in those days beset the path of the youth aspiring for an education."
—*Chicago Inter-Ocean.*

QUEER STORIES FOR BOYS AND GIRLS. 12mo, $1.00.

"A very bright and attractive little volume for young readers. The stories are fresh, breezy, and healthy, with a good point to them and a good, sound American view of life and the road to success. The book abounds in good feeling and good sense, and is written in a style of homely art."—*Independent.*

BOOKS BY HOWARD PYLE

BEHIND THE GARDEN OF THE MOON. A REAL STORY OF THE MOON ANGEL. Written and illustrated by HOWARD PYLE. Square 12mo, $2.00.

Out of the truth that great deeds are achieved and high character moulded by entire spiritual consecration, rather than by direct and interested effort, the author has evolved a winning and delightful piece of fanciful fiction, and has illustrated it copiously in his happiest and most characteristically poetical vein.

THE MERRY ADVENTURES OF ROBIN HOOD OF GREAT RENOWN IN NOTTINGHAMSHIRE. With many illustrations. Royal 8vo, $3.00.

" This superb book is unquestionably the most original and elaborate ever produced by any American artist. Mr. Pyle has told, with pencil and pen, the complete and consecutive story of Robin Hood and his merry men in their haunts in Sherwood Forest, gathered from the old ballads and legends. Mr. Pyle's admirable illustrations are strewn profusely through the book."—*Boston Transcript.*

OTTO OF THE SILVER HAND. With many illustrations. Royal 8vo, half leather, $2.00.

" The scene of the story is mediæval Germany in the time of the feuds and robber barons and romance. The kidnapping of Otto, his adventures among rough soldiers, and his daring rescue, make up a spirited and thrilling story."—*Christian Union.*

THE BUTTERFLY HUNTERS IN THE CARIBBEES

By Dr. EUGENE MURRAY-AARON. With 8 full-page illustrations. Square 12mo, $2.00.

" Our author only reproduces the incidents and scenes of his own life, as an exploring naturalist, in a way to capture the attention of younger readers."
Chicago Inter-Ocean.

JUST PUBLISHED

THE KING OF THE BRONCOS

AND OTHER TALES OF NEW MEXICO. By CHARLES F. LUMMIS. Illustrated by VICTOR PÉRARD. 12mo, $1.25.

A charming collection of stories of life and adventure in the Southwest. The last story, " My Friend Will," is a masterpiece, with a brainy moral for adult as well as juvenile readers.

A NEW MEXICO DAVID

AND OTHER STORIES AND SKETCHES OF THE SOUTH-WEST. By CHARLES F. LUMMIS. Illustrated. 12mo, $1.25.

" Mr. Lummis has lived for years in the land of the Pueblos; has traversed it in every direction, both on foot and on horseback ; and it is an enthralling treat set before youthful readers by him in this series of lively chronicles."—*Boston Beacon.*

STORIES FOR BOYS

By RICHARD HARDING DAVIS. With 6 full-page illustrations. 12mo, $1.00.

" It will be astonishing indeed if youths of all ages are not fascinated with these ' Stories for Boys.' Mr. Davis knows infallibly what will interest his young readers."—*Boston Beacon.*

HEROES OF THE OLDEN TIME

By JAMES BALDWIN. Three volumes, 12mo, each beautifully illustrated. Singly, $1.50; the set, $4.00.

A STORY OF THE GOLDEN AGE. Illustrated by HOWARD PYLE.

"Mr. Baldwin's book is redolent with the spirit of the Odyssey, that glorious primitive epic, fresh with the dew of the morning of time. It is an unalloyed pleasure to read his recital of the adventures of the wiley Odysseus. Howard Pyle's illustrations render the spirit of the Homeric age with admirable felicity."
—Prof. H. H. BOYESEN.

THE STORY OF SIEGFRIED. Illustrated by HOWARD PYLE.

THE STORY OF ROLAND. Illustrated by R. B. BIRCH.

THE BOY'S LIBRARY OF LEGEND AND CHIVALRY

Edited by SIDNEY LANIER, and richly illustrated by FREDERICKS, BENSELL, and KAPPES. Four volumes, cloth, uniform binding, price per set, $7.00. Sold separately, price per volume, $2.00.

Mr. Lanier's books present to boy readers the old English classics of history and legend in attractive form. While they are stories of action and stirring incident, they teach those lessons which manly, honest boys ought to learn.

THE BOY'S KING ARTHUR **THE BOY'S PERCY**

THE BOY'S FROISSART **THE KNIGHTLY LEGENDS OF WALES**

FRANK R. STOCKTON'S BOOKS FOR THE YOUNG

"His books for boys and girls are classics."—*Newark Advertiser.*

THE CLOCKS OF RONDAINE, AND OTHER STORIES. With 24 illustrations by BLASHFIELD, ROGERS, BEARD, and others. Square 8vo, $1.50.

PERSONALLY CONDUCTED. Illustrated by PENNELL, PARSONS, and others. Square 8vo, $2.00.

THE STORY OF VITEAU. Illustrated by R. B. BIRCH. 12mo, $1.50.

A JOLLY FELLOWSHIP. With 20 illustrations. 12mo, $1.50.

THE FLOATING PRINCE AND OTHER FAIRY TALES. Illustrated. Square 8vo, $1.50.

THE TING-A-LING TALES. Illustrated. 12mo, $1.00.

ROUNDABOUT RAMBLES IN LANDS OF FACT AND FICTION. Illustrated. Square 8vo, $1.50.

TALES OUT OF SCHOOL. With nearly 200 illustrations. Square 8vo, $1.50.

"The volumes are profusely illustrated and contain the most entertaining sketches in Mr. Stockton's most entertaining manner."—*Christian Union.*

THINGS WILL TAKE A TURN

By BEATRICE HARRADEN, author of "Ships That Pass in the Night." Illustrated. 12mo, $1.00.

One cannot help being fascinated by the sweet little heroine of this tale, she is so engaging, so natural; and to love Rosebud is to love all her friends and enter sympathetically into the good fortune she brought them.

JULES VERNE'S GREATEST WORK

"THE EXPLORATION OF THE WORLD."

"M. Verne's scheme in this work is to tell fully how man has made acquaintance with the world in which he lives, to combine into a single work in three volumes the wonderful stories of all the great explorers, navigators, and travelers who have sought out, one after another, the once uttermost parts of the earth."

—The New York Evening Post.

The three volumes, in a set, $7.50; singly, $2.50.

FAMOUS TRAVELS AND TRAVELLERS. With over 100 full-page illustrations, maps, etc. 8vo, $2.50.

THE GREAT NAVIGATORS OF THE XVIIIth CENTURY. With 96 full-page illustrations and 19 maps. 8vo, $2.50.

THE GREAT EXPLORERS OF THE XIXth CENTURY. With over 100 full-page illustrations, fac-similes, etc. 8vo, $2.50.

JULES VERNE'S STORIES. UNIFORM
ILLUSTRATED EDITION

Nine volumes, 8vo, extra cloth, with over 750 full-page illustrations. Price, per set, in a box, $17.50. Sold also in separate volumes.

MICHAEL STROGOFF; or, THE COURIER OF THE CZAR, $2.00. **A FLOATING CITY AND THE BLOCKADE RUNNERS.** $2.00. **HECTOR SERVADAC.** $2.00. **A JOURNEY TO THE CENTRE OF THE EARTH.** $2.00. **FROM THE EARTH TO THE MOON.** $2.00. **DICK SANDS.** $2.00. **THE STEAM HOUSE.** $2.00. **THE GIANT RAFT.** $2.00. **THE MYSTERIOUS ISLAND.** $2.50.

NOAH BROOKS'S BOOKS FOR BOYS

THE BOY SETTLERS. A STORY OF EARLY TIMES IN KANSAS. With 16 full-page illustrations by W. A. ROGERS. 12mo, $1.25.

"A volume that all spirited boys will admire; its descriptions of frontier life are accurate and exciting."—*Boston Saturday Evening Gazette.*

THE BOY EMIGRANTS. With illustrations by T. MORAN and W. L. SHEPPARD. 12mo, $1.25.

"It is one of the best boys' stories we have ever read. There is nothing morbid or unhealthy about it. His heroes are thorough boys, with all the faults of their age."—*The Christian at Work.*

THE FAIRPORT NINE. By NOAH BROOKS. Illustrated. 12mo, $1.25.

"It is full of wild adventures and boyish tricks, but its general tone is wholesome and manly, and while its young readers will find it sufficiently 'jolly' they will get no harm from it."—*Philadelphia Times.*

THE NORSELAND SERIES

By H. H. BOYESEN.
NORSELAND TALES. Illustrated. 12mo, $1.25.
BOYHOOD IN NORWAY: NINE STORIES OF DEEDS OF THE SONS OF THE VIKINGS. With 8 illustrations. 12mo, $1.25.
AGAINST HEAVY ODDS, AND A FEARLESS TRIO. With 13 full-page illustrations by W. L. TAYLOR. 12mo, $1.25.
THE MODERN VIKINGS: STORIES OF LIFE AND SPORT IN THE NORSELAND. With many full-page illustrations. 12mo, $1.25.

The four above volumes in a box, $5.00.

TWO BOOKS BY ROSSITER JOHNSON

THE END OF A RAINBOW. AN AMERICAN STORY. Illustrated. 12mo, $1.50.
"It will be read with breathless interest. It is interesting and full of boyish experience."—*The Independent.*
PHAETON ROGERS. A NOVEL OF BOY LIFE. Illustrated. 12mo, $1.50.

BOOKS OF ADVENTURE BY ROBERT LEIGHTON

JUST PUBLISHED

THE GOLDEN GALLEON. A STORY OF QUEEN ELIZABETH'S TIME. Illustrated. 12mo, $1.50.

PREVIOUS VOLUMES

OLAF THE GLORIOUS. A STORY OF OLAF TRIGGVISON, KING OF NORWAY, A. D. 995-1000. Crown 8vo, with numerous full-page illustrations, $1.50.
THE WRECK OF THE GOLDEN FLEECE. THE STORY OF A NORTH SEA FISHER BOY. Illustrated. Crown 8vo, $1.50.
THE THIRSTY SWORD. A STORY OF THE NORSE INVASION OF SCOTLAND, 1262-65. With 8 illustrations and a map. Crown 8vo, $1.50.
THE PILOTS OF POMONA. A STORY OF THE ORKNEY ISLANDS. With 8 illustrations and a map. Crown 8vo, $1.50.

"Mr. Leighton as a writer for boys needs no praise, as his books place him in the front rank."—*New York Observer.*

NEW AMSTERDAM EDITION

HANS BRINKER; OR, THE SILVER SKATES. By MARY MAPES DODGE. New edition, with over 100 illustrations by ALLEN B. DOGGETT. 12mo, $2.50.

Mrs. Dodge's ever-popular story will appeal afresh to old and new readers in this handsome new edition. The pictures not only adorn the book most attractively, but illustrate it in the highest sense, reflecting the spirit of the text most admirably, and depicting the Dutch scenes and characters with great fidelity. They are the result of a special journey to Holland, undertaken by the artist in order that he might visit, in person, the places where scenes of Mrs. Dodge's story were laid.

W. O. STODDARD'S BOOKS FOR BOYS

DAB KINZER. A STORY OF A GROWING BOY.   SALTILLO BOYS
THE QUARTET. A SEQUEL TO DAB KINZER.   AMONG THE LAKES
WINTER FUN